HELL CAT
OF THE HOLT

MARK CASSELL

HERBS
HOUSE

Published in Great Britain in 2017 by Herbs House
An independent publishers

1

For more about this author
please visit www.markcassell.co.uk

ISBN 978 0 9930601 4 4

Printed and bound for Herbs House

First Edition

For those who have seen things

HELL CAT
OF THE HOLT

A novella in the Shadow Fabric mythos

CONTENTS

holt – noun, dialect, archaic

A wood or wooded hill.

<u>Origin</u>: Old English, of
Germanic origin; related to
Middle Dutch *hout* and
German *Holz*, from an
Indo-European root shared
by Greek *klados* 'twig'.

A STORY I HEARD

From sunlight to darkness in mere seconds. Squealing tyres, shrieking metal. And silence ...

Alfred opened his eyes but only blurred light greeted him, jagged and confusing. The stench of burnt rubber and damp foliage clogged his nostrils. He coughed and an ache raced through his brain. Seconds dragged as his vision sharpened the sunset. The sound of tinkling glass lanced his eardrums, and he tried to move. His seat belt restricted him.

Then he remembered: Martha hadn't worn her seat belt.

Thank the Lord she was still with him, wide-eyed and pretty as always – her senior years had been so very kind. Regardless of not wearing her restraint, she looked fine if a little dazed.

Somewhere above them, birds chirped. Those shrill cries drilled into his head. He winced.

Often, he would tell Martha – *remind* her – to fasten her seat belt, and she would always respond that she never found them comfortable. This went back to the mid-70s when a Road Traffic Bill was put forward in the House of Commons, coinciding with those 'Clunk Click Every Trip' TV commercials. He remembered the fuss she made when they became compulsory to wear if the car had them fitted.

"What a silly idea!" she had said at the time. "Strapped in like children."

The right side of his head hurt like hell. He rubbed his face and his hand came away wet, and red. The rest of his body felt fine other than a few familiar aches; for the past decade, his body had woken up to all sorts of discomfort. Yet he could not complain, he was more able-bodied than the majority of his peers and, moreover, his mind remained sharp.

The windscreen was a patchwork of cracks. His door window, however, was unbroken, beyond which he saw the cat – again. Not your average domestic cat, but much larger. It now crouched in the darkness of thorny bushes, blending with the shadows. Could it be a panther? Dear God, really? He had heard of black cat sightings in the area, although shrugged them off as ridiculous urban legends.

The bloody thing was the reason why he'd crashed. He had been the one driving, Martha beside him, when the large cat had bounded across the road: black hair glistening, eyes reflecting the sunset like cooling embers; a sudden dark streak across the tarmac. Alfred had swerved.

And here they were: his car a wreck, mangled bonnet around the trunk of a looming oak.

With rubber fingers, he released his seat belt. The metal clasp smacked the central pillar. Shifting sideways, still aware of the cat's presence, he looked at his wife. Being such a law-abiding English gentleman, he had soon given seat belts little thought and found himself clunking and clicking. They were not in any way uncomfortable as Martha had protested. Several years ago, he read somewhere that on the 40th anniversary of Clunk-Click, over one-hundred thousand lives had been saved. He wondered what the tally was now, himself and Martha included in those numbers.

"It's okay," he whispered and took Martha's hand.

It was relatively easy to clamber from the wreckage, and even when they were both clear he didn't once lose his grip on her. They stood looking at the Toyota's crumpled bonnet and mashed grill. Steam hissed. Wispy phantoms crawled up the bark.

The cat – the panther, whatever it was – was no longer nearby. A quick scan of the surrounding trees and shrubs and tangle of brambles, revealed nothing. Still that warmth filled him. Fear of the cat or anger at crashing, he could not tell.

Martha wasn't saying much, nor could he blame her. It was he who had been driving; he was to blame, taking a shortcut through country lanes at a time of day where the low sun bleached the world, pale and bright. Martha had been talking about their plans for after they'd returned home.

"Don't get me wrong," she was saying, "I've truly enjoyed our weekend, it's just I miss having time away from home. I'd like us to book another break, further away and for longer. Not just one week but perhaps two. We need to make the most of these years, Alfred, while we're still in good health."

He saw her point; if only she could see his when it came to wearing that seat belt. Sometimes he annoyed himself and he doubted that he would ever give up thinking of her safety.

Now he was walking with her, away from the car wreck. And that cat. The sunset blinked through the branches of the autumnal canopy and they eventually came to a stream cut between the immense oaks. Without pause, they stepped into the water. Coldness soaked through to his toes, and he and Martha cleared the stream in two strides. His shoe slipped on the embankment. Martha found it no trouble and remained silent as he composed himself on the other side.

The air damp, the ground swampy, their trek through the woodland became more a zigzag path, avoiding lichen-coated rock and ivy-clad boulders. Some of the boulders were broken, gaping like jagged yawns. Years of forest growth covered each one, and although some were as large as houses, they were dwarfed by the surrounding oak trees.

Over the last few years, Alfred had taken to each day with appreciation. Life was for living. Enjoying. It was sad there were those who took it upon themselves to end their own lives. What of the driver heading towards the cliff without any intention of braking? Did they, from home to final destination, bother to wear a seat belt? Were they at such an emotional low they clicked the belt into place out of simple habit as opposed to an ironic view of their safety during the oncoming journey? Maybe they wished to avoid any entanglements with the law, and if they considered such things with apparent lucidity then was it not possible to bring themselves out from their most desperate hour?

If only things were as simple as the pleasant stroll he and Martha were now taking.

Parallel to them, the cat broke the shadows between a scattering of smaller rocks. Its eyes again reflecting the sunset. Not at all urban legend but *real*, as sure as his own heartbeat. Incredible. Crisp leaves whispered beneath its paws as it kept pace with them.

A small part of him knew he should be afraid, but …

Thinking back to the accident, Alfred squeezed Martha's hand. Still she said nothing, nor did she return his small sign of affection. Was it affection? Guilt, most likely. The sun had been low in the sky and he had reduced his speed accordingly, but he should have seen the cat sooner. The next moments were lost to darkness … and now he was walking with Martha, walking away from that darkness.

Just as it had then, the beast leapt across their path. Hair glistened, muscles rippled. It bounded in front and froze between tree trunks on the edge of deepening shadows. A flurry of leaves swirled. The impressive beast huddled in a place where rays of red sunshine failed to penetrate.

The air seemed to shrink in Alfred's throat, and he and Martha jerked to a standstill. He must run, return to the car wreck. He had to call the police, an ambulance … Run, run away …

Those red eyes, not reflecting the sun at all but glowing from an inner fire, locked on to his own. A heat surged through his body, similar to that which filled him earlier in the day on the south-east coast; a rare warmth which arrived with a strange October, the two of them appreciating both the weather and the other's company. He was lucky. *They* were lucky.

From behind them, leaves rustled. Getting louder. Voices too.

Alfred turned.

Two police officers approached between the trees, twigs snapping.

"Sir," one of them shouted. "Stop there!"

Alfred looked back towards the cat. Its eyes burned, blinked once, and it tilted its great head. Then it darted off. Nothing more than a dark streak in shadowy folds, it vanished. A chill rushed through him. His fingers and toes numbed and his breath plumed before him in a lazy cloud. He dragged his eyes from the swaying foliage, from what looked like quivering shadow, and peered over his shoulder. His head throbbed.

All he could do was let go of Martha's hand.

One policeman already stood a short distance from Alfred, while the other staggered to a halt further away.

A silence deepened the gloom.

The officer closest to Alfred opened his mouth to say something, but his colleague's strangled words stopped him. Alfred frowned and wondered what they were both staring at. He followed their gazes, looking down at his feet.

Blood peppered his shoe and soaked into the earth. Next to that was Martha's hand.

"Martha," he said, "you should have worn your seat belt."

MY NAME IS ANNE

I'd heard the stories and read the articles, but despite growing up under my grandparents' care in the village, I had never once seen the Black Cat of Mabley Holt myself. And that had been frustrating. After all with its population of little more than one hundred, you would have thought I'd get at least one glimpse. As I grew older, even though the sightings were mostly reported by adults, I resigned myself to the idea it was something that happened only to little girls – if at all.

Kind of like seeing fairies.

Grandad claimed he'd seen the Black Cat, and that was all he spoke about after the accident. Three days later he'd died of a broken heart.

That had all happened last year.

A little piece of me had also died when I lost first Gran in that car crash, then Grandad. I took a modicum of comfort from the fact that I'd lived back home with them, in the room I'd had as a kid, for about a year before the accident, providing me with recent memories to cherish.

Orphaned at birth and an only grandchild, a failed marriage and unashamed cat lover, my life had seen its share of ups and downs. I'd meant to have been living there again only temporarily, but now they'd both gone, I guessed it was a good enough place to start a new chapter in my life.

So here I was, stepping out of my family home …

I zipped up my coat. The fresh morning rushed into my lungs, and I squeezed a pocket; I had a habit of forgetting my purse. It was in there. The front door clunked shut and I gave it a push to make certain it was locked. I walked down the short path that led to the road. No pavement, just the cracked tarmac of the country lane beyond an iron gate, which had remained open since the 1980s, rusted and tangled with brambles.

A blue Ford sped up the road.

"Speed bumps," Gran always used to say. "The road needs speed bumps."

Since the funeral, it seemed both their voices echoed a little too often. Especially over Christmas; how that house had echoed memories. Now spring approached, I still heard them.

Back in the autumn I'd lost them both, then five months later I'd lost Murphy, my own black cat, my little buddy.

I walked past the houses of my only two neighbours – each hemmed in by overgrown leylandii hedgerows – and headed up the road. It was a ten-minute walk to the local shop, along a winding lane with too many potholes. I needed some milk but figured I'd grab it on the way back from my walk.

I wanted to look for Murphy for the umpteenth time in less than a week.

My stroll followed a roadside ditch filled with the mulch of leaves and rain. Eventually, I rounded the last bend that led to a row of terraced cottages, beyond which was the shop.

The elderly lady who lived in one of the large houses further along the road stood in front of a telegraph pole, pinning something to it. Her name was Rose, one among a handful of residents who'd remained in Mabley Holt throughout my twenty-year absence. She stepped back from the poster of another missing cat.

My pace slowed.

She'd fixed her laminate below my own.

It had been six days since Murphy had left through the cat flap, having licked clean his bowl and not returned. My stomach churned a now-familiar sadness.

Rose's down-turned mouth twisted into a weak smile when she saw me approach. I knew my mouth mirrored hers.

"Yours too, huh?" I said.

She nodded, her jowls wobbling slightly. "Helix has been gone four days now."

"Almost a week for my Murphy." I eyed his photo. It was the one I'd taken of him in front of a roaring fire the previous Christmas back when I'd lived up in Birmingham. My photo was in colour whereas Rose's was in black and white, of her black and white cat.

"I still put fresh food out for him," Rose said, "near the cat flap, just in case."

"Me too." I wondered how old Helix was.

"And biscuits."

I wondered if I'd ever see Murphy again.

"And water," she added.

Another car shot up the road. Again, too fast. When they finally completed the bypass, it should reduce the number of vehicles using the village as a cut-through. Too many times since Murphy's disappearance I'd considered the possibility of his fate beneath speeding wheels.

"We can only hope," I told her. "Keep looking, keep hoping."

As I continued along the road towards where the pavement finally began, I of course scanned the last ditch, the last hedge, and the fields beyond, just looking for a tiny furry body. What I'd do should I actually find him there, I had no idea.

I shivered and made fists in my pockets; I should've worn gloves.

A black 4x4 was parked with two shiny alloy wheels over the pavement — probably the only off-roading the vehicle ever saw. Some of the smaller cottages didn't have front gardens let alone a driveway or garage, and several had large vehicles which didn't help the parking situation. Often, I'd overhear neighbours complain. I usually kept my car on the driveway, however it was currently gaining the attention it deserved after I'd ignored the Engine Management System warning light for too long. Having it breakdown on me a few days ago had brought on more tears than it deserved, but it just topped everything off.

The last twelve or so months had been incredibly sad: leaving Birmingham, a beautiful home and an incompatible husband, to return to my grandparents' house all the way down in the south-east. The life I thought I wanted was just not for me so I had come back to the room I had as a little girl, welcomed with as much love as ever. Gran had made extra fuss, and she never tried to hide her joy at having me once again under their roof.

I reached the shop and paused, wondering if I should go in; I wanted to head up the road, wanted to look for Murphy near the church. Voices drifted from the gaping door beside me. A stack of bread crates had been left just inside the threshold: Hovis, Kingsmill, all household names that reminded me I should add bread to the list. I'd write a shopping list in my head and later forget most of it when I was actually in the shop. I suspected that would happen again now.

"… stuff is everywhere …" It sounded like one of my neighbours, Harriet. Her voice carried like gunshots to chase me as I headed up the road. I could not be arsed with her right then. I wasn't in the mood.

At the junction, the familiar smell of oil clung to the air – Mabley Holt residents had oil tanks in the garden because British Gas had never got around to connecting pipes to the village. To the left was the kiddie's playground, and beyond that a rusted National Speed Limit sign gave way to another lane that wound towards the main road for Sevenoaks. Off to the right sat the church with its spire lancing into the overcast sky.

I rounded a ragstone wall that began at ankle level and soon towered above me, leading into the graveyard. By now it had to be 7.30 a.m. This had always been my favourite walk – there was something about treading the crooked and often overgrown path between moss-coated headstones and broken grave markers ... just *something*.

When I first returned to Mabley Holt I'd considered getting a dog for a walking companion, extra company alongside Murphy, but I preferred cats. Not only that, I didn't think Grandad would have much liked the idea. Both he and Gran were cat lovers too, and had been more than happy when I'd come home with Murphy. There's a strange kind of knowledge behind the sneaky intelligence of a cat, and that's something I'd always admired and respected.

Murphy, where are you?

The air turned colder as I stepped into the shade of the church itself. White moss peppered the stonework, the walls chipped with years of abuse from the elements. This particular wall, I'd always noted, was battered more than the others and I assumed it was because it faced the open fields. From its place atop the hill, the church overlooked the valley that at this time of year was a mix of browns and greens. Today, patches of fog drifted at the edge of the far woodland. Soon there'd be a hint of rapeseed yellow to prove that spring was here, but not quite yet.

I continued walking towards a rusted fence that marked the edge of the holy grounds. Dry leaves crunched beneath my shoes as I slowed my approach to the fence. I stopped beneath the drooping limbs of an oak whose roots had devastated what perhaps were the first graves to have been laid. The wind bit my cheeks as I curled fingers around the cold and rusted iron. It gave a little beneath my grip and made a grinding sound in the ruined paving. My breath plumed as I squinted across the expanse of churned earth, out towards a copse. Little more than a collection of perhaps a dozen sizable trees, the copse stood in the centre of the nearest field.

Where those trees once stood proud, their trunks and branches were now shrivelled, blackened. Burnt.

The ground surrounding the trees was barren, typical for the time of year, but in places scorched. The trunks and branches were black from what I guessed must have been a fire. Strange thing was it hadn't been like that the day before when I'd walked up here. Of that, I was certain.

Maybe there'd been a lightning strike last night – even though I'd not heard a storm. Maybe it had been some pyromaniac youths. Using that word, youths, reminded me of Gran.

The jagged trunks of several trees reached up to the sky like black claws. Whatever the cause, the fire had only burned long enough to take out the copse and spread no further. Aside from the scorch marks, there were deep cracks and rifts that splayed out from the blackened tree line. It reminded me of those pictures of the barren ground in Ethiopia where, as a kid, I'd first witnessed sun-baked earth and famine, sad eyes and pot-bellies.

A rustle above made me jerk upright, my neck clicking. I stared into the gloomy thatch of branches. Something dark, fleeting, teased my peripheral vision. I tried to follow whatever it was and saw only twigs and branches quivering. Perhaps it was a squirrel, or … or something larger than a squirrel.

Murphy?

I moved and my shoe caught on a cracked paving slab. As I went to step away, my coat snagged on the fence and ripped.

Whatever had been in the branches had gone.

Nothing. No Murphy.

When I went home, I forgot to go in the shop.

Typical me.

I knew at some point I'd seriously have to get on with my contracted work, and it was already way past midday. Freelance accountancy had been my thing since leaving Uni, but recently I hadn't been getting much done. It seemed I allowed myself far too many tea breaks where I'd not actually make any tea, and instead wander off into the village and the surrounding fields in search of Murphy. Procrastination was always an issue, and right then I was hungry and had little in the cupboards in the way of lunch.

I was just considering going back out to get that shopping, when a screech of tyres and a crash put a stop to my intentions.

I rushed to the window and bumped the sideboard, knocking off a photo frame. It cracked when it landed by my foot. Such a clumsy arse. Ignoring it, I pulled aside the net curtain to look out.

Just past my neighbour's house, a red van sat crooked in the ditch atop flattened bushes with its crumpled bonnet against the telegraph pole. Steam poured from the front grill. The driver, a good-looking guy with one tattooed arm, clambered out. His eyes were wide. He didn't immediately inspect the damage, instead he paid more attention to the field beyond the trees and bushes past the wreck.

I wedged my feet into my shoes, stomping them in for a few steps to properly get them on.

Clive, my elderly neighbour, was already out of his house by the time I made it onto the road. I wrapped my cardigan around my chest, hugging myself and wishing I'd grabbed a coat. After the funeral, Clive had been there for me. Indeed, he and his wife, before she'd passed away, had been good friends with my grandparents. Today, it was no surprise that he wore his mustard-yellow jumper. I'd never once seen him without it. When I lived here as a kid, I'd always see him wearing it – I honestly wondered if it was the same one. Even in summer, he'd wear it without rolling up the sleeves, and in winter, he'd not wear a coat.

"I'm okay, thanks," the driver was saying to him as he ran a hand over his vehicle's roof. "Van's not."

"You sure you're okay?" Clive held an empty shopping bag in one hand and his house keys in the other.

The driver again glanced over the hedges. A mist crept along the far edge of the field, curling through tufts of grass down where a stream wound into the expansive woodland.

"Damn thing came from nowhere," the man said.

"What?" Clive demanded. "What did you see?"

"The thing darted from the bushes."

"Yes, but what?"

I believed I knew what the man was about to say.

"A big black cat."

I wasn't surprised and immediately thought of Grandad. As a kid, a number of long-living residents of the village often spoke of how they'd seen the Black Cat skulking through the fields. One old lady once claimed her late husband fired his shotgun at it. Point-blank range, apparently. No harm befell the cat.

"Look at my van!" the man said.

"Anne," Clive said, his eyes narrow, "are you okay?"

I nodded, knowing I held my mouth open, and quickly closed it.

The man looked at me, then eyed his van. "Had an accident."

I wanted to say, "I can see that", but that would made me sound like an arse. That wasn't my style. My throat was dry.

The man walked round the front of the vehicle and stroked the bonnet. "Still haven't finished paying it off." He dug in his pocket and pulled out a mobile phone.

"Shopping?" I said to Clive, pointing at the bag. It was an obvious question, I realised that, and I had no idea why I asked. Perhaps it was to distract myself; I was still thinking of Grandad in hospital, adamant he'd seen a black cat. *The* Black Cat.

"Yes, I need a few things," he said and glanced up the road. "Have you found little Murphy yet?"

I hated that question. A friend from Birmingham had phoned that morning asking precisely that. I gave them both the same answer: "No, not yet."

My neighbour's gaze drifted over my shoulder, and I turned to watch the van man lean against his side door. He was speaking on his mobile. Clive and I walked a short distance away to allow the man some privacy.

I wanted to talk about the Black Cat, my Grandad. Everything.

Eventually, Clive murmured, "Said he saw the Cat."

"What do you think?"

"I think he's telling the truth."

"Why?"

"Because I saw it, too."

"You did?"

"About a minute before the crash." With his shopping bag, he motioned across the fields. "Over there, down near the stream."

"Yeah?"

"Yes."

I didn't believe there was a Black Cat, or the 'Black Cat of the Holt' as Grandad said just before his heart finally broke. I couldn't believe such a beast roamed the local countryside. In truth, the idea scared me. Imagine if … if the Cat had got Murphy. Perhaps the Cat had eaten him.

My stomach churned at the thought.

"That fog is heavy," he said, "and it's coming in fast."

It clawed along the edge of the woodland, drifting in layers.

"I need to get to the shop," Clive said and started walking. "See you."

Me too, I thought, but I didn't go with him. I went back indoors, grabbed my coat and eyed the cracked photo of Gran and Grandad. I still didn't bother picking it up.

Before Clive had even made it a dozen steps up the road I was outside again, such was his slow plod. By now, the van man sat in the driver's seat. I wondered if I should at least offer to make him a tea or a coffee. Then I saw him pop open a can of drink, a Coke or Dr Pepper maybe.

He looked fine.

Off I went in the opposite direction to Clive, heading down towards the stream.

At this time of year, the stream would be deep enough to be a river. The sound of tumbling water intensified as I walked off the field into the woodland, following the slope that led down to the stream. The river. The damp air, earthy and salty, filled my lungs. Around these parts of the village, mossy rocks and ivy-clad boulders dotted the landscape, some as small as a shoebox, whereas others, without exaggeration, could be compared to the size of a house.

A large portion of rock had broken away and slid into the deeper part of the river to form a kind of waterfall. Gnarly roots pushed out from the muddy slope, growing up and over several large rocks. Overhanging branches dangled into the water, creating ripples. Layers of mist teased the water bank, not as thick as I'd suspected.

The cross-hatching of overhead branches creaked. For a moment, I expected to see whatever it was that had spooked me earlier. Nothing there. Just gloom.

No Murphy.

Not that I expected to see him up a tree. I'd never known him in a tree, but then again, I'd never known him to go missing. I was there for a different kind of cat. What was I even doing? This could be dangerous.

Something behind me rustled in the leaves, I turned and—

My leg shot sideways. I slid, landed in the mud, and slipped further down the embankment.

A coldness soaked through my jeans, to my skin. My hands raked the mud … down I went … and cold water rushed over me. Freezing. I choked and coughed and sputtered, my arms flapped, my hands slapping the surface. The back of my head went under, my ears bubbling. Luckily my face didn't go under. Rocks bit into my back and my bum. My legs kicked the tangle of reeds. It was like a dozen hands wrapped around my ankles, keeping me under. Cold water rushed down my throat and again I choked and coughed. I scrambled, desperate to grab something, anything.

Finally, my slick hands gripped a branch. Only just. I lurched and fell back as though a tide swept me beneath its surface.

My wet hand lost its grip.

I turned over, still kicking, still flapping my arms. My head smacked a rock. Light and colour and darkness blinded me and I went under; my whole head this time. Chunks of broken rock lined the bottom of the river, and as I tried to get my feet beneath me, I saw what looked like cave paintings. Reds, yellows and blues painted on the rocks. No time to make any sense of it.

I lurched upright, desperate to grab the branch again. It was as though the water was deeper than it really was.

The branch. Got it. Tight.

Water rushed over me. I swallowed some and choked. Cold and bitter.

Beside me, up the bank, there was movement. A blurry image of someone running from the fields, then sliding in the mud, nearer and nearer the river. An arm reached out and for an absurd moment all I saw were those rock paintings again. I kicked and thrashed and grabbed the arm. Strong, hairy.

The man yanked me up. His fingers pinched my skin as I jerked upwards. All I saw was his woolly hat and a firm jaw. He slipped, and embarrassingly I landed on top of him. Coughing, I glared at the churning water, expecting to see something reaching for me. My breath came in gasps and I pushed myself away from him. My cheeks warmed despite my cold skin; I'd landed on top of the poor man.

"It's okay," he said. "It's okay."

"But, I saw …"

He glanced at me as we both stood. I guessed he was a hiker.

"I saw something down there," I told him. My legs felt like jelly.

"What?" He snatched off his black coat and draped it over my shoulders. He looked at the landslide, watching the water tumble over and around the rocks. "What did you see?"

His coat smelled of clean laundry and I felt guilty as I wrapped it tight around my shoulders, hugging myself. My teeth chattered and all I could taste was that bitter water. "I … I don't know."

He raked his stubble. His brown eyes were as dark as the muddy water. They were sad, though.

"Lucky I was nearby." His voice was soft. "You okay?"

I nodded, feeling as dumb, as they say, as mud. My hands were slick with the stuff. Plus, I'd broken a nail; like I cared about that. The murky mix of bubbles and debris made lapping noises against the bank of tree roots and rock. How I even managed to see the rocks at the bottom and those markings I had no idea.

"Recently," he said, "people around here have been seeing a lot of weird stuff."

Again, I nodded. I was such an idiot; I couldn't believe I'd fallen into the river. My teeth felt furry, gritty, and like the true lady I was, I turned my head aside and spat. It didn't do much for getting rid of that awful taste. "Excuse me."

"S'okay." He laughed. "Can't imagine it tastes nice."

"Nope."

"Mucky."

"Yeah." I rubbed my hands together. It made little difference to the chill, but I kind of felt better. I had to get home.

"You local?" he asked.

"Yeah."

"Me too."

Again, I looked at him. I didn't recognise him.

"Come on," he added, "let's get you home. Is it far?"

"Not at all." I jerked my head in the direction of the field behind us. "On the edge of the village. You'll see my house once we get away from the river."

He wiped his muddy hands down his trousers. He wore combats and big boots.

"I reckon," he said, "you'll be taking plenty of that water with you."

I looked at his wet trousers. "You too. And your coat's gonna be soaked."

He waved a hand. "Nah, it's cool."

I went to move away from the embankment and staggered like I was drunk.

He reached out and gripped my upper arm. Firm. "You good?"

"Yeah."

"I'll walk you home."

"You don't have to."

"Yeah." His smile warmed his face, but failed to warm me. "Yeah, I do. I'm Leo, by the way."

"Anne," I said and wiped my face with his sleeve. "I'll wash this coat for you."

"You don't have to."

"Yeah, I do."

We stepped up the bank and headed for the edge of the field, the barren ground slick with mud.

"I've not long moved into the village," he told me. "Been here since last summer. Gone by fast."

My shoes squelched around freezing toes as we headed for the main road and my house. "I kind of keep myself to myself, to be honest," I told him.

"Me too." Again, I thought how troubled he looked.

I glanced behind us, back down towards the river. "Have you seen the Cat, too?"

He took a moment to answer. "I've seen a lot of things."

"A big Black Cat? Some guy earlier claimed he saw a panther."

Leo shot me a curious look.

"I've also heard that pet cats have been disappearing," he said.

"My Murphy."

"I've seen your posters."

"I miss him."

"Of course you do." He dropped his gaze to his feet. "You went down there to look for it, didn't you? The big Cat, right? The panther?"

"Stupid, huh?"

"Of course not," he said.

"Curiosity." For the first time, I thought how terrible it would be if Murphy had been killed by this so-called panther. I hoped to hell that wasn't the case.

"I'm sure Murphy's okay," he assured me. "Maybe stuck in someone's shed."

"It's been almost a week."

The rest of the way, which wasn't too far, was in silence. The closer we got to my house, the more embarrassed I felt. I was *such* a clumsy idiot. By the time we reached it, I noticed the crashed van was empty. The driver had most likely gone up to the shop. Or, knowing Clive, he was bending the man's ear about the hiking trails around the local countryside. He and his wife, Janice, used to hike a lot with my grandparents.

"That doesn't look good," Leo said, gesturing at the wreck.

"Nope." Given my clumsiness down at the river and meeting Leo, I'd forgotten all about the accident. "It happened earlier. The driver said he swerved out of the way of the Black Cat."

The muscles along his jaw rippled. His head rocked forward and back, slowly. He didn't say a word.

"Thanks for walking me."

"No problem," he said without looking at me. Instead, he focused back on where we'd come.

"And thanks for the coat," I added, "I'll wash it."

"It's okay," he said and held out his hand, "I'll do it."

I slipped it from my shoulders and handed it to him, feeling so pathetic it annoyed me.

He rolled it up and mud dripped on one of his boots. "See you around, I'm sure."

"Yeah." I almost added, *I'd like that*, but managed to catch myself. I dug in my soaking pocket for my house key.

Leo turned and started walking down the lane.

"Do you think we should call the police?" I asked.

He stopped and looked back. "No."

"Why not? We should tell them about the Black Cat." It was the kind of thing Harriet would have done by now. If not, perhaps even Clive.

"I don't think that'll help matters," Leo said, and pulled his hat down tighter on his head. "The police can't do anything."

Before I could protest, he turned and strolled off. Water dripped from him and his big boots left mud in his wake.

I unlocked my door, thinking of his last words.

Harriet shuffled aside as I slid the bottle of milk across the counter. How was it she seemed to be in the shop every time I was? And I didn't go in often. Her presence made me feel tiny – especially her great bosom. What was it with older ladies like this? Even her voice was massive.

"And," she was saying, "that's when I noticed the black stuff all over the back steps."

Hadn't she been talking about the black stuff earlier? Even though it was late in the afternoon, absurdly I wondered if she'd been in the shop all day. The shop assistant, a young girl with a nose stud and whose name always escaped me, threw me a quick smile. She looked apologetic and bored.

"Just this please," I said and glanced at Harriet. This was the first time I'd spoken since falling into the river and as I spoke, I could still taste the bitter water.

"Have you noticed any of the fungus?" Harriet asked me.

Moments like this, I hated. I had to talk, what if I said something stupid? These kinds of thoughts came at me in waves. Sometimes I'd be the most confident person you'd meet, other times not. What if the shop assistant laughed at me? A cool sweat prickled my forehead.

"No," I whispered. It was the truth. Kind of. I thought of the burnt and black trees I'd seen earlier that morning.

"It's everywhere." Her eyes were wide. "I bet there's some of it outside, out the back of the shop, already creeping across the walls."

"It's probably just a weed," the young girl said.

"It's more than that. When you touch it, it gets everywhere." She clutched her purse to her chest and gave me a crooked smile. "See …" She pointed at my boot, "… it's everywhere."

Mud caked my boot. My shoes were soaked from falling into the river, and earlier I'd thrown them out onto the back step to dry out. The boots I now wore had hardly been worn and already they were streaked in mud – dark mud, almost black though. I didn't say anything, my mouth drying up like I hoped my shoes soon would. I kept my eyes on my purse as I pulled out a pound coin.

Harriet started talking again.

My cheeks burned by the time I stepped out onto the street, and the woman's voice faded behind me. I snatched up my collar and headed home. As I passed Murphy's photo on the telegraph pole, I glanced at it while keeping my pace.

Nearing my lane, the fog thickened as though eager to join twilight.

The sound of an approaching vehicle from behind made me move closer to the bushes. Headlights speared the fog and pushed a haze of white into the sky. A roadside rescue truck passed and it made me think of the crashed van – if that was for the guy who'd wrecked his van, I wasn't impressed with the response time. It made me think of how he'd been certain he saw the Black Cat.

Big cats, small cats, whatever. All I wanted was to find Murphy.

Harriet's cottage was on the other side of Clive's, with an immaculate garden that shamed ours. Sickening, in truth, even though this past winter had been cold and wet. She was right, the apparent black fungus covered her driveway. Also, peculiar dark vines encased a section of the wall.

Whatever the stuff was, she just needed weed killer – I should probably add some to my next shopping list in case it spread into my garden.

For a moment, I considered going for a longer walk than I had earlier that morning. Not really looking for Murphy – who was I kidding? Sure, I'd be looking for him – but I could do with clearing my head. However, I had to get on with some work, even though there really wasn't much of the afternoon left. It looked like I'd be working through the evening.

As suspected, the rescue truck pulled up alongside the crashed van where the man was climbing out. He looked like he'd been sleeping.

A glance into Clive's garden and I saw him crouched at his front door, placing two empty glass bottles on the doorstep. This I marvelled at. I remembered my grandparents used to have a milk delivery every morning, way back when I was a little girl. I didn't realise it was still a thing.

Clive watched me approach my gate and smiled.

"Hi," I said.

"Hello, Anne."

I trundled up the path, key in hand … and I saw smudges of the black stuff over the lower door panel. Not much, but enough for me to pull a tissue from my pocket and wipe it off. It was kind of like charcoal. Not really a fungus at all. Although my knowledge of fungi was zero if you didn't include those closed-cup mushrooms I cooked with.

Inside, the first thing I did after removing my coat was pick up the cracked photo frame I'd knocked off the sideboard earlier. Reminding myself I should do some housekeeping, I straightened it along the line of dust where it once stood.

Behind the sideboard and in the thin shadows down near the skirting, something seemed to be wedged. It looked like card or a piece of paper.

I rolled up a sleeve and reached down behind the unit. Although awkward, I managed to pinch an edge. It hissed against the wall as I brought whatever it was into the grey light from the window.

A perforated sheet of notepad paper.

It was aged yellow and gritty with dust. I didn't recognise the rushed, uppercase handwriting, so I assumed neither Gran nor Grandad had written it. Without taking my eyes off the two scrawled words, I stabbed the light switch beside me.

BLOOD
BREATH

The sound of shattering glass, cracking and smashing, stole me from a deep sleep. I squinted into the blue light of my bedroom. When you wake from a sudden sound, your first thought is whether it was real. You're unable to comprehend what it was, where it came from and whether you heard it in the first place. That was me right at that moment. Had I heard it or had it been in a dream?

I lifted my head from the pillow, listening hard. I held my breath.

A scream made my stomach twist. Inhuman.

It was feline.

Murphy?

I leapt up, kicked away the duvet and scrambled for the curtains. I wrenched them aside and pressed my forehead to the cold glass. The contact froze my skin, and if I wasn't already fully awake, I was now.

On the street below, in a haze of fog, two shapes hurtled across the road, one after the other. Two cats. Neither one was Murphy. Both looked like tabbies. The pair began mewling, a painful sound that sent a shiver up my neck and into my scalp.

Outside Clive's house, halfway down the path, shards of milk bottle glass reflected the moonlight. His porch door hung wide, gently swinging. I stretched my neck to see if he was out there, but he wasn't from what I could tell. When I looked back at the cats, they were no longer there. All that remained was a faint white mist that rolled across the garden.

Several seconds passed as I waited for movement. Where was he?

Still nothing.

Why was his door open?

Perhaps he was in trouble.

I snatched up my clothes, caring little for fashion. I even grabbed a hat and wedged that over my messy locks. In no time at all, I had my boots on and ran out into the street.

The cold stole away my echoing footsteps as I came out onto the quiet road. Dirt and twigs covered the tarmac. No sign of the cats.

I circled the fence and trees that separated our gardens, and came to Clive's front gate. The iron was cold to the touch and it squeaked as I pushed it. I avoided most of the broken glass, their lethal curves reflecting a tiny moon. Some of the smaller pieces crunched as I headed for his porch. Both doors hung wide, offering only a dark gloom from within. I hoped he was okay.

"Clive?" I called into the darkness. My voice sounded strange on the night air.

The silence remained.

I prodded the doorbell button and it buzzed through the house. No one answered. Nor could I hear footsteps.

But the doors were open. Why? I didn't know if I should go in. What if he was unable to come to the door? Perhaps he'd hurt himself. Or worse.

Without a choice, I entered the porch. Palm flat, I nudged the inside door. It creaked and swung inward to thump against something. I stepped over the threshold and past a pair of Wellington boots. One had toppled over, the sole caked in mud. Clumps of it peppered the lounge carpet. A stale smell washed over me as I made my way further into his home, reinforced by the heating that I suspected was cranked up. Making my way through his house without invitation made me feel like an intruder. The moon's silvery-blue rays crept through the open curtains to blend with several lamps that offered pockets of yellow light.

There was Clive.

Although seated in an armchair beside a dim lampshade, the shadows seemed to fold in around him. For the first time I saw him without that mustard-yellow jumper of his. Instead, he wore a dressing gown. Grey, curly hair sprouted from his thin chest in sporadic tufts over a photo frame he clutched in arthritic knuckles. He was still, his head slightly slumped. My heart lurched; my immediate thought was that he was dead.

Slowly, I approached …

He looked up. "Anne?" His voice was barely audible. Thank God, he wasn't dead.

With his mouth down-turned, his eyes were tiny; he looked like the old man he truly was. His hair stuck up in all directions.

"Clive," I said, "everything okay?"

He hugged the photo closer to his chest.

I navigated around a tumbled pile of books and got closer.

"Clive?" I lowered myself onto the sofa beside him and the stink of body odour wafted over me.

Despite the heat, his bottom jaw quivered as though he was cold. I had no idea whose photo it was he held.

"She died last year," he told me. "She was everything to me."

I assumed he spoke of his wife, Janice. She sadly died just before I moved back to Mabley Holt. A lovely lady who always offered a smile when I saw her. Gran and Grandad used to spend a lot of time with their neighbours. Although with Harriet, not so much.

"Oh, Clive, I'm so sorry." What to say to that kind of thing? I'd always been useless in these situations, never knowing the best way to reply.

He lowered the photo.

The wooden frame was chipped and dusty along the top, the photo itself faded and crinkled, possibly sun-bleached. Although it was in black and white, a radiant sunshine was evident in their squinting grins. It featured a much younger Clive and his wife standing before a railing, with the sea stretched out behind them. He wore sharp trousers and highly-buffed shoes, and she wore a dress and held a small handbag.

"Janice," he said and lifted his sad eyes to look at me.

"She was always kind to me, when I was a kid."

"She was kind."

A sharp crack sounded across the room, near the bay window.

I started, sitting upright. "What was that?"

"No idea." He placed the photo on the sofa. His knees clicked as he pushed himself up and stooped. It made him appear much smaller than he actually was.

I stood and edged round the sofa, treading carefully past several cans of cheap lager. There was a torn TV mag screwed up underneath a dinner plate. A fly took off from mouldy bread crusts and buzzed past my head.

Again, that crack. I jumped and the back of my leg hit the side unit.

In the bay window, dark patterns that looked like fungus had crawled across the glass. Even as I watched, it splayed and reached into the wooden corners. The glass cracked like a web. More fungus grew.

"Clive …"

"I see it."

"What the hell is it?" I thought of the way I'd seen it around the village. "Why's this stuff everywhere?"

When I turned back to him, something shimmered behind him in the doorway: a fleeting shift of grey and white, something in the shadows. It was like someone walked past in the hallway that led to the kitchen.

Clive straightened up. "She's there, isn't she?"

The more I looked, the less I saw. Just the hallway and the faint beams of moonlight pressing through the blinds to spotlight the kitchen sink.

"I don't—" My tongue stuck to my teeth.

Again, glass cracked behind me.

I spun round.

In the lower section of the bay window, that black stuff sprouted even thicker and crumbled onto the window sill. For the briefest of moments in the gloom, I saw an image in the broken glass.

A face. One I recognised.

An older face than in the photograph Clive had held a moment ago: Janice.

Her image was somehow etched in the window, smeared in the fungus. Yet the more I looked, the more it morphed into the jagged cracks and black filth it really was.

Wasn't it?

Had I actually seen his wife's face?

I was just tired.

The next morning, I woke early from a broken sleep of blanket wrestling. The slightest of sounds, whether imaginary or not, kept yanking me from sleep. And every time I'd jerk awake, I saw again how Janice's image shifted in the broken glass and fungus.

It was of course ludicrous. No way had I seen an apparition of Clive's dead wife. It was all down to tiredness, stress. Let's face it I'd been piling a lot on my shoulders: losing my family and allowing work to stack up, and more recently having car problems, and now Murphy going missing.

Now I was seeing the impossible.

I needed more than sleep, I needed a holiday.

Although I doubted it, I hoped Clive had a better sleep than I did. If not, perhaps he was having a long lay-in. Yet I could not shove aside thoughts of him still on the sofa clutching the photo frame. I'd left him there after he insisted I should leave. He'd not said anything more about seeing a ghost.

Ghosts. Damn it. Totally ridiculous.

The remainder of the morning went by with my head in my work, and somehow, I got through enough to be pleased with. This time of year was always busy; it wasn't long until my clients' tax returns had to be completed. I was good at numbers, but they still did my head in. Incredibly, I even managed to eat some lunch. Mid-afternoon took me to the point where I became cross-eyed. However, I was more than happy with how much work I'd completed.

Time to focus on something else, which of course led me outside to search for Murphy. Patches of fog and a gradually darkening sky proved how far away spring really was.

As I passed Clive's house, I saw he hadn't cleared his path of broken bottles. Nor had he cleaned up the fungus, or indeed done anything about the cracked bay window. For a moment I considered knocking to see if he was okay.

I didn't.

Further along the lane and I paused in front of Harriet's immaculate garden. Evidently, she'd prepared it for the daffodils that would soon erupt from her pristine borders that ran either side of those gleaming paving slabs. The fungus was no longer there, and I assumed she'd spent the day gardening. Beside her front door, the frayed rope dangling from an iron bell swayed. It looked like she'd even painted the bell.

My foot sank into the ground when I turned to walk off. I'd not stepped in mud; it was that muck. Black clumps dotted the tarmac in the direction of the bridleway across the road. The way it was spaced out, it looked like footprints.

Or, more to the point, *paw* prints. Just dark, black dirt. It was coincidence that it looked like paw prints, right?

But … they were as large as my fist.

Thinking of how it had spread in Harriet's front garden and across her drive, I wondered if there was any in my garden now.

From behind the houses, something banged. Followed by a series of crashes and clatters that echoed into the quiet countryside. It sounded like garden furniture collapsing, and scuffing concrete. But from whose garden? I couldn't quite tell.

I ran to my gate and up the path, cutting across the driveway. Whatever the commotion, it was escalating. Definitely in Clive's garden. I bounded past the wheelie bin and rushed through the shiplapped gate, thumbing the latch in one move without losing a step. In my garden, I slammed against the fence and tiptoed, hooking fingers over the wood.

"Clive?"

He stood in the middle of his patio staring into the bushes that led out to the fields beyond our gardens.

Cats.

I saw the curling tails of a couple vanishing through the bushes and up over the back fence. The sounds of clambering and scratching claws on wood faded. Beyond the garden, rushing into the fields, were perhaps a dozen of them. A white one, a ginger. Grey. Black and whites. All hurtling across the muddy field. There was a black one – Murphy! – but it was too small, the tail too slender.

"Murphy?" I yelled. My heart raced with them.

No Murphy.

Clive still hadn't looked at me, and we both watched them vanish into the tree line that separated the churned field and the river. A haze of fog teased the ground, drifting through the grass.

"He wasn't with them," Clive said without turning.

His garden was a mess of cracked plant pots and scattered furniture. A chair lay in the flower bed.

"I didn't see him." His hair was as unkempt as it had been the previous night. Unsurprisingly, dark loops of wrinkled skin hung beneath his eyes. "I always look out for him."

"But ..." I said.

"Where did they all come from?" he said for me.

"Yeah, where—"

"I've no idea." He looked at me. "They were all suddenly in my garden."

"Why?" And why wasn't Murphy with them?

"Like they appeared from nowhere," he added.

"Whose are they?"

He shook his head, and looked back across the field. I couldn't be certain but maybe I saw a final tail vanish into the foliage.

We stood there in silence for a minute or two, perhaps it was only seconds, but evidently we had the same questions and confusion going around in our heads. I thought of how he'd acted the night before. His face was unreadable, his brow wrinkled more than usual.

Finally, I said, "How you feeling this morning?"

"She speaks to me." His expression didn't change.

For the briefest of moments, I wondered who he spoke of. Of course ... it was Janice. I'd seen the apparition of his dead wife in the window, hadn't I? Even though I had no explanation for it. Could I have hallucinated?

He shook his head as though reading my thoughts. "You saw her. I know you did."

A coldness spread down my spine.

"Janice," he said.

"I have to go," I told him. I'm not the tallest of people and tiptoeing to see over the fence was starting to kill my ankles. Plus, I had to get away from him. I didn't want to face this madness. *His* madness. "I have a lot to do, and seeing ghosts is not helping." I felt my cheeks and ears warm.

"I don't understand it either, Anne." His eyes were tiny.

As he turned away, I dropped back onto my heels. My feet pressed into the soil, sinking like my stomach now the excitement of almost finding Murphy had passed. I calmed my breath, forcing my anger down. I didn't want any of this. I'd told Clive I had much to do, yet I knew I wasn't going to do any of it. Well, at least not the working section of that to-do list; I would head out and look for Murphy, out in the direction of where those other cats had gone.

Hope. Something I'd begun to cling to.

The walk of perhaps ten or fifteen minutes turned up nothing. No Murphy, nor any other cat. Nor did I see any of that black stuff anywhere. My thoughts were of Clive. Perhaps his grief had pushed him to the edge, and he believed she was talking to him. He'd said he'd been talking to her, so I assumed he'd also seen, just as I had if only for a moment, reflections in windows. I then felt bad for running off like that. I'd snapped at him and the poor man was still grieving, clearly going senile in his elderly years. He'd lost his wife and still mourned, now claiming to see her.

But I'd seen her, too. Hadn't I? Were we both hallucinating?

For the first time, I thought maybe it was the black stuff. Could it be a kind of hallucinogenic fungus? While chewing on these thoughts, somehow I'd walked from the field and through the trees. Seeing the river up ahead of course made me think of that embarrassing moment when I'd slipped in and Leo had rescued me. I wondered where precisely he lived in the village, and what his connection was to all that was going on.

I kept further away from the water this time, heading for the shallower stretch. Compared to the day before, I could now see the bottom: clumps of reeds and heaped rock. No coloured markings though. Had I imagined that, just as I'd imagined seeing Janice's ghost? The further I walked, the more I realised that it had dried up, which was a little strange given the time of year. Plus, there were more rocks that had slid down from the opposite bank.

Although I'd often walked down here, especially since Murphy's disappearance, I didn't recognise it. The landscape had changed. Quite drastically, in fact. I couldn't even tell where I'd fallen. Finally, I got to something that most definitely wasn't there the day before.

One rock speared the ground as though it had risen upwards, slick and glistening with streaks of mud … and unsurprisingly that fungus.

I skirted several tree roots and walked towards it. How had this happened? It was like it had burst up through the ground. I ran two fingers along the cold, damp surface, careful not to touch the black filth. From this angle, between jagged pieces of rock, I saw where I'd scrambled up the muddy bank when Leo saved me. Again, all those rocks had not been there. Could there have been some kind of earthquake? It wasn't a common occurrence in Britain, and when there were quakes they were usually harmless. But this … this had to have been an impressive ground shift. If there had been one close to my house, I certainly would have felt it. It would've been the talk of the village. Even if it had happened at night, it certainly would have woken me up.

A cold wind bit my face.

The now-dry reeds were blackened, which immediately brought to mind the scorched copse I'd seen from the graveyard overlooking the fields. Everything looked burnt: trees roots, rock, and even the mud itself.

Somewhere close by, a twig snapped. I squinted over a low rise in the woodland, off into a cluster of undergrowth. Beyond a fallen tree, in shadowy foliage, there …

My heart jolted.

… there was the Black Cat.

No more than fifty metres away.

I held my breath.

Even from that distance, I could see the muscles ripple along its flank as it strode past a mossy boulder. It didn't look like a panther or a puma or anything like that. It had a round, soft face, with what looked like a bald patch on one side of its head. Those great paws pressed into the leafy floor and its head swayed in time with each mighty stride. It slowed to a stop.

I dared not move.

With a casual neck roll, it turned its immense head. Ears back, eyes wide that burned a deep red, it scanned the woodland.

A beam of sunlight fell across its mouth.

Those lips … they seemed to be stitched together. Thick and glistening, perhaps even sweaty, stitches. Its hairless chin was blistered and scarred around the uneven weave of tatty cords.

That great beast fixed me with its fiery gaze.

I wanted to run, to sprint, to get out of there as quick as possible but my feet refused me. I breathed, slowly, not even wanting my chest to move for fear of encouraging the Cat to advance.

Silence squeezed me, choked me, and it was as though the air had thinned.

The Cat hunched. Then bounded forward.

My heart pummelled my ribcage but still I couldn't budge.

It leapt over the fallen tree, straight for me.

Finally, my legs obeyed and I turned and charged back up the slight incline. Out into the field where the grass whipped my trousers. Every step sent a hammer to my skull. Thick mud clumped my boots making my sprint so damn difficult.

I didn't want to look back, couldn't.

It was close. I knew it.

My coat made ridiculous wispy noises as I pumped my arms back and forth, propelling myself across the field. This had to be the fastest I'd ever sprinted in my life. I knew I'd never make my house, as I imagined the beast growing even larger, impossibly huge, bounding after me.

I ran, and the darker everything became …

My heel slipped.

I stumbled, my heart pulsing in my throat. Somehow, I managed to remain upright. Still running …

And that gloom pressed in like a premature twilight; darker, thicker, to block out the bushes far ahead, my house.

A growl – close! – from behind made me turn.

A split-second glance: the Cat. Hair rippling, big and bold. Crimson eyes.

That growl was like an engine.

I looked ahead, sprinted faster. My legs burning, my lungs screaming. Yet … it felt as though time slowed. The mud, the earth, the ground, sucked at my boots. I mentally shouted at my feet to take me the hell away from there. Run. Faster.

No response.

I slowed. No. I had to keep running. Go.

Slower. It was like I ran in slow-motion. Perhaps I was dreaming.

That growl intensified.

I didn't want to, but I turned to look back again. Why? I had to run. My stride had stopped. That was the only movement I could afford, as though I was trapped by quicksand.

The Cat no longer advanced, standing perhaps ten metres away. A smell, a mixture of swamp water and burnt toast wafted towards me. Its nostrils flared. The side of its head where its flesh was blistered and bald, glistened black filth. It slid down the side of its jaw, and dripped to the ground. Tiny coils of smoke rose from where it burned the grass.

I waited for it to pounce.

Death had chased me. I hoped to God it would be painless.

Nothing.

Those eyes had dimmed, yet its look seemed more curious than anything. There was no evil there, no ill intent. Its head tilted, and slowly those eyes closed. As the fiery tinge in its pupils vanished, I felt my feet move.

Finally.

Light returned, creeping back around me. Pushing away the darkness.

Although slightly numb, my legs moved and I stepped back from the Cat. The retreating shadows stole the Cat away, too. It was like it vanished, shrinking into the fading layers of darkness.

I continued to step back and I pressed into bushes. Twigs and leaves scratched my coat. Now at the far edge of the field, not too far from my house, I realised I'd managed to run further than I thought. All that remained of the Black Cat's presence were paw prints that had blackened the grass. Curls of smoke caught on the breeze, bringing with it a subtle whiff of burning.

I stood there, my breath loud. I wrapped my arms around myself.

Was I going insane? What was going on? It had to be the fungus, it was making me see things. But the paw prints were proof I wasn't.

Daring myself to see the Cat again, I squinted into the distance. The trees swayed above a drifting fog. Nothing else. No Black Cat.

What. The. Hell?

I jogged alongside the hedges with the uneven ground threatening to steal away my unsteady legs. Somehow, I managed to get myself over the stile that led back out onto the lane. When I neared my garden and rounded the corner, there was Leo crouching on the other side of the road, just a little way along from the public bridleway. Wearing that woolly hat of his, he scribbled in a notebook; frantic pen movements beneath grim concentration.

"Leo," I said as I approached. My throat was raw. Tears prickled my eyes as I held it all back. "I've just seen the Cat."

"This village is getting more and more insane," Leo said as he looked up and snapped shut his little notebook. The blue of twilight was fast approaching, making me wonder how long I'd been down by the river. It seemed to close in on the pair of us, reinforced by the shrubs and trees. Unlike the gloom from moments ago, this was natural, safe.

Normal.

But I no longer lived in a normal world.

"I saw it," I said again.

He nodded.

I crouched and watched him run a hand along the ground. Black patches dotted the cracked tarmac.

"Don't touch it!" I said. "It's a fungus, hallucinogenic or something."

He chuckled, but there was no humour in it. "No. No, it's not."

Even the stones, half buried in the earth between thick weeds, were black. His palm came away with dark smears, like charcoal.

A wind flicked hair in my face and I hooked it from my mouth.

"It's everywhere," I said. "What's going on?"

He pulled his hat tighter over his ears and added, "It's so much more than that."

Together, we stood.

"Anne, you know there's always been Black Cat sightings in these areas, but this ..." He gestured to the black streaks. "This takes it up a level."

"What does that mean?" I hadn't meant to raise my voice.

He didn't say anything, only looked at me with those large brown eyes. I guessed there was sympathy there.

"Leo," I said as he looked away, "I've just been chased by a fucking big black cat. It's *the* Black Cat."

He slid his notebook into a pocket, keeping his eyes fixed on the black stuff at our feet. "This is all connected."

"And speaking of lips," I shouted into his face, "that Cat's lips were stitched closed and half its head was burnt and blistered and scarred." My eyes prickled and I blinked away pathetic tears that threatened to push me over an edge I absolutely refused to pass.

Leo placed a hand, gentle and warm, over mine. He softly squeezed my fingers. "It's okay, you're safe."

"What's happening?" Again, I pretty much shouted it. Was I becoming hysterical?

He offered a soft smile.

I inhaled and closed my eyes. He squeezed my hand again, then let go. I breathed out, long and loud.

Eventually, I opened my eyes and said, "Sorry."

"Don't be. I know precisely how you feel. Not too long ago, I was yanked into all this weird shit."

"Really?"

"Yeah, and I'm still piecing it all together. Trying to, at least."

I gestured to the ground. "This black stuff is everywhere, we should inform the environmental agency."

"They can't do anything." He shook his head. "This is so much more than that."

"What is it?" I wanted to ask more about the Cat. So many questions hurt my head.

"This black stuff, as you call it," he rubbed it between finger and thumb, "is a kind of residue. It proves the veil between our world and ... and *another*, has been torn."

I laughed. "Yeah, right."

"What have you seen, Anne? Tell me."

"I've just seen the Black Cat of the Holt, I know that."

"And you're sure about that?"

"Yeah."

"A second ago you mentioned the possibility of a hallucinogenic fungus."

"I did, but I know what I saw."

"So, you believe?"

"Yes." I thought about how that impressive beast had chased me. "It vanished into a strange grey fog. No, it was like the shadows opened up or something."

His nod was enough to convince me he believed me. He asked, "How d'you reckon that's even possible?"

I had no idea. "And its mouth was stitched together." I remembered how those stitches appeared sweaty. "And its eyes were like fire."

The smile that pushed into his face made me want to scream at him. Again, I had to calm myself. "It was as though it vanished into thin air."

"And the shadows?"

"The shadows moved without any reason. Kind of messed with my perception, you know?"

Leo looked away and squinted into the darkening sky.

"What you're seeing aren't the shadows you think they are, it's the veil shifting, traces of the Shadow Fabric."

"What?"

"A sentient darkness that exists in varying forms and allows entities to move between worlds." He said it with such conviction.

"Nonsense."

"It is quite literally the Fabric of Reality."

"And what do you mean … *entities*?"

"Precisely that."

"Are you talking about ghosts?" I demanded. This was ludicrous. "Spirits?"

"Demons, too."

"This is insane." Although I said that, I thought back to what I'd witnessed at Clive's house.

He chewed his lower lip, then said, "That's what I once thought."

"How do you know all this shit?"

"I've dealt with this kind of thing before. And I learnt a lot from a good man. I've stayed in Mabley Holt because this place seems to be at the heart of it. There are things buried in this village. Secrets … and more."

I looked past him, out into the fields down by the river. Out of the corner of my eye I saw him follow my gaze. The way he said all this convinced me that there was much more going on.

"You want to know what I was doing down by the river when I rescued you?" he asked.

I kicked at the clumped mud on my boots. "Yes," I mumbled, "yes, I do."

"Want to come back to my place?"

That question did not make me feel weird. I know it should've done, but instead I somehow knew I could trust him.

In silence, we walked up along the bridleway, stepping around muddy puddles and precarious tree roots smoothed out from years of walkers. As we neared the end of the path, and came closer to the lane beyond, he cleared his throat.

"Since last year," he said, "I've been trying to piece together the history of Mabley Holt. Strange things have been happening here for centuries. It all centres around those rocks out there in the woods. What no one realises is that many of them are markers. Kind of grave markers ... but for demons, devils."

I laughed. "You expect me to believe this?"

"I *need* you to."

"This is absurd."

Even though I said that, the more he spoke the more I believed in what he was saying. I realised that I had in fact seen Janice's apparition, and hadn't been hallucinating after all.

"They're recognised as containment stones," Leo explained, "to hold at bay a buried demon."

"Okay, so if all this is true ..." I found it almost hilarious that I was taking this seriously. "... why, or indeed *how*, are the demons buried here? How is that even possible?"

"They exist in two places, and need to rebuild themselves. See it as though the empty shell of their body is buried beneath or between a series of containment stones. And on the other side of the Fabric their actual consciousness resides. Banished, in a way, beyond this world."

"I suppose they need to connect?"

"Yes, precisely."

"How does that happen?"

"Flesh and blood. Sometimes just a touch of the living, sometimes the breath of a living being here on Earth."

When he said that, I immediately thought of the piece of paper I'd found at the back of my grandparents' sideboard. Something I'd totally forgotten about until that moment.

"Blood?"

He nodded.

"And," I added, "breath?"

His eyes widened, his head tilted. It reminded me of how the Black Cat had moved its head, just before it closed its eyes and vanished.

"Where did you hear that?" he asked.

"I …"

He frowned.

Should I tell this man? This stranger? I hadn't known him long. Did I want to tell him stuff about my family?

"It's okay," he said, "you don't have to tell me if you don't want to."

I paused, and instead told him, "Some of those stones looked like they've moved. There are more out in the countryside, more than before. And they look like they've risen from the ground."

He remained silent as we made it out onto the road.

"How is that even possible?" I demanded.

The sound of an approaching vehicle made us stop to watch headlights spear the twilight shadows – normal shadows, I hoped. We watched the car shoot past, its occupants no doubt clueless as to what was happening here in the village. Red brake lights vanished round the bend.

I looked back at Leo. Could I tell this man of that one curious thing I'd found in my grandparents' home? If I did, then it felt as though I'd let him into my world. My messed up world. It had been that way for a while now. Now, even more so. His was too though, by the sounds of it. If I could believe him. And I did believe. Everything.

So, I told him about what I'd found. The two words.

Again, he tilted his head and I held his gaze.

"Yes," he said, "blood and breath."

Leo lived in one of the two cottages I'd often walked past on my search for Murphy. Both gardens were as overgrown as my own, although on his driveway sat a silver BMW. It had a registration plate from last year, hiding beneath accumulated grime that I suspected was just as old.

Inside his home, sparse and contemporary furniture dotted the place. This, for some reason, surprised me. An ugly yellow coffee table sat in the middle of the lounge. An aroma of coffee disguised a lingering stale smell, and I wondered how long it had been since he'd opened a window. I followed him through to a back room which suited him more than what I'd seen of the rest of the house.

He switched on the light and gestured for me to sit in a threadbare armchair beside a window without curtains. From what I saw of his rear garden in the swiftly-falling twilight, it looked just like the front.

I didn't sit down.

Books of varying age covered a small computer desk in the corner. A laptop sat askew in the middle of a bunch of papers. Some newspapers, too. Empty Budweiser bottles filled the wastepaper basket beside a swivel chair.

The most dominant thing in the room was an impressive world map which almost filled a wall from floor to ceiling. Cryptic diagrams were pinned across it and coloured string connected several locations, surrounded by photographs and printed images. One was of an amber mask, another of a Mediterranean island. There was a close-up of a group of suited men talking in a restaurant, and even a hazy photograph of a jungle tribe. The latter had an arrow pointing to it in thick black marker pen, and scribbled over the Atlantic Ocean were the words: DEVIL'S SKULL. From that, a smaller arrow pointed to what my limited geographical knowledge made me see as Peru. I couldn't be certain because most of that continent hid behind curled notebook pages containing chunks of text. Great Britain was a mess of coloured pins, and so beside it was a larger map of the British Isles and another of Kent, highlighting Mabley Holt itself.

"What is this?" I asked as I approached it.

Pinned beside the map of Mabley Holt were two photocopied images: one of an hourglass which appeared to have a leather strap attached to it, and another of an ornate knife.

"What does it all mean?" I looked at him. He'd been watching my reaction all this time.

"This is my life," he said.

This was chaos, that's what it was. On the desk, askew with the laptop, an acrylic painting half hid under a book. It was square, not much larger than the book itself.

"What the hell …?" I snatched it up. "What the hell is this?"

I couldn't believe what I was looking at.

His jaw muscles rippled and he breathed out, his face giving away nothing.

It was a painting of a woman underwater, wearing shoes and a familiar coat. She had her face against a rock at the bottom of the river.

"It's me …" I whispered.

In the painting, the rocks had traces of reds and yellows, like some kind of underwater cave painting. Just like I'd seen the moment before Leo had rescued me. In the corner, there was a large pair of boots evidently running – the motion was captured with incredible talent.

"You painted this?" My tongue stuck to the roof of my mouth. "How did you know what I saw? I didn't tell you what I saw!"

Leo said nothing, only stared back at me.

"Answer me!" I threw the canvas back on the desk and it landed beside an ancient-looking tome titled *Necromeleons*. I had no idea what that meant and didn't care.

"That was painted last week," he said.

"Impossible. You must have painted it after you pulled me out of the water. You went home and painted it then, yeah? That's what happened."

"I didn't paint it."

"Who did then?" My cheeks burned.

"A lady called Pippa, a fine artist."

"Who the hell is Pippa?"

"She's my neighbour."

"What?" I laughed. "Next door?"

"Yes."

"I want to meet her. Now." I knew I was getting hysterical again, but this was all getting too much.

"You're not ready."

"What the fuck does that mean?" This guy was seriously pushing my buttons. I grabbed the painting again, my knuckles white.

"Anne, honestly, there's something about Pippa that isn't entirely … um … normal."

"And what does that—?"

There was a knock on the door. Soft at first, then frantic.

Leo's brow furrowed and he straightened up. "Stay here," he said and strode into the other room.

I threw myself into the chair and groaned. The stupid chair was not even comfortable; thin cushions allowed the wood to press into my bum. This was all getting far too crazy for me. I glared at the canvas, at the way the artist had painted those markings. It was precisely what I'd seen.

"Insane," I said.

Leo's voice boomed through the house: "Holy shit, man!"

I leapt up and tossed the painting onto the chair, and jogged from the study. My legs ached. I went through the dining room and—

Leo had a man's arm around his neck, staggering into the lounge. Whoever it was had blood caked over his yellow jumper and on his neck and face. It slicked his grey hair flat.

"What happened?" Leo demanded.

My stomach twisted as I approached.

"Clive?"

INTERLUDE (PIPPA)

Last summer

Pippa hated deadlines. She packed too much into the day and she knew it.

Kneeling, she yanked aside the carpet and a cloud of dust plumed. She coughed. The underlay crumbled as she pulled further and rolled it halfway across the room to lean against an easel and a box of acrylics. As always, getting carried away with any project at hand. She intended to dedicate an entire week to an approaching deadline and to finish the studio. Her *studio*. She found it pretentious to call it that, but now that she received paid commissions it was time to do this.

She coughed again and leapt to the window. Whatever she'd inhaled clung to her tongue like bitter chalk. As she opened the latch, birdsong washed into the room and the countryside stole away the dead air. Beneath an overcast morning and beyond her garden, fields stretched across the Kent hills like a stitched blanket of varying shades of green.

She moved from the window to face the room.

Something had once burnt the floorboards: scorch marks zigzagged the timber, some curled to create arcs that disappeared beneath the roll of carpet.

Weird. Two years since buying the place and she had no idea they were there. Crouching, she rubbed the gritty timber. Her palm was smeared black as though she'd been sketching with charcoals. Rubbing her hands together made the stuff crumble away like black breadcrumbs.

She stood and pain lanced her temple. Agony shot across her forehead, into her brain, and darkness pressed in from the corners of her eyes, tighter, tighter and …

Cold air rushed into her lungs. She staggered. Twigs snapped beneath her shoes.

Where was she?

Below the brilliant slice of moon, branches creaked and leaves hissed on a wind that stabbed her clothes. The wet smell of undergrowth and foliage overwhelmed her. Her knees weakened, her legs buckled, and she fell. Her fingers pushed into the soggy ground, freezing. She groaned. A myriad of colours swept across her vision.

"What—?" She was somewhere outside, in the fields behind her cottage perhaps. Yet it was so cold. This surely couldn't be a summer's night. And it had been morning a second ago.

Fragments of stone squatted in the shadows; mossy and jagged, half buried. Gravestones? Maybe she wasn't near home at all. But there were no other markers and certainly no churchyard, only looming trees and that sliver of moon.

The darkness beyond deepened, shifted. A silhouette broke the shadows.

A woman approached.

Her dress whipped around thin legs and bare feet, movements slow and jittery. It was as if she waded through water.

Pippa pushed herself backwards, her shoes digging into the earth.

The moon cast a silver halo around the woman's unkempt hair, leaving her face in shadow. Closer, closer … and Pippa pushed herself back further, and further.

The rough bark of a trunk dug into her spine.

Still no more than a silhouette, this woman, this *phantom*, reached out a slender arm. The moonlight reflected from young skin, her fingernails chipped and raw, skin bleeding. Closer.

She pressed icy knuckles against Pippa's forehead.

A short scream tumbled from Pippa's quivering lips and echoed through the trees.

Something rumbled, deep, grinding. Black lines scorched the ground, singeing the leaves and twigs and even the earth itself. Cracked and broken stones pushed through the earth. Silhouettes flickered and shimmered between trees. More phantoms. All dressed in rags, some clutching shreds of fabric to thin bodies. All featureless and blank, hidden in the shadows.

Those fingers still pressed her forehead, numbing her brain. Darkness swarmed her, the images of the women blurring. Blending and churning.

Pippa jerked upright, eyes wide.

Back in her studio, a low evening sunshine poured through the open window. The comforting smell of paint clung to the air.

In front of her stood five easels, each supporting a canvas displaying her bold style. A smaller one balanced on the roll of carpet. Paint of every colour smeared her hands, her clothes. She tasted acrylics on her lips.

One canvas was of an oak tree that towered over the bloodied bodies of men, their clothes torn – perhaps even *clawed* – open. Blood soaked the grass. From a twisted branch above dangled a hanging woman dressed in little more than rags, her head angled in a noose. Another was of a market square in an unfamiliar village, focused on the thrashing body of a woman tied to a wooden post. She was on fire and screamed into the night. The flames illuminated both the surrounding crowd and billowing smoke. Several onlookers writhed on the ground, their heads a bloody mess against uneven paving. The other paintings depicted similar scenes of women dying; stabbed, drowned, beheaded. This last was particularly nasty.

She'd dedicated an entire day to this insanity; a day that should've been for commissioned work. Why couldn't she remember painting these?

The smallest canvas that rested on the roll of paint-spotted carpet was unfinished. The least menacing, it depicted a wall of looming rock, moss-covered and ancient. Across the leaf-strewn ground, dark clumps of mushrooms or fungus darkened the shadows. No death scene here. She recognised it; she'd recently been there. Yes, on one of her long inspiration-searching walks across the fields.

Her head pounded and she was hungry, tired.

She snatched up the bottles of acrylics and brushes that were scattered about the floor and threw it all in to cartons. She couldn't keep this stuff; she'd have to buy more. She had work to do, deadlines to meet.

She glanced at each painting. Finally, her gaze dropped to the floorboards, to those scorch marks. She had somewhere to go, somewhere to visit: that sheer-faced rock wasn't too far.

So much work to do.

Deadlines.

She hated deadlines.

EVERYTHING CHANGED

Leo bustled into the kitchen, half-carrying, half-dragging Clive. Blood and black filth smeared the poor man's hands and face. His bottom jaw quivered, his eyes darting all about the room. I helped guide the old man to the sink. Leo ran hot water and squirted washing-up liquid into the bowl. The smell of fresh lemon filled my head.

"Good as anything," Leo said when he caught my disapproving look.

I guessed it would be better than simply using hand wash, so I grabbed a cloth and turned to Clive.

"Janice …" He pushed my hand away. "Janice!"

I thought of the image I'd seen at his window, and that he believed he could speak with the apparition. Given all that I'd recently learnt, I now believed him.

"I woke up with this blood everywhere," he sputtered and finally allowed me to help clean his hands. "I don't understand."

"What happened?" I asked as I searched for cuts. There were none. "Whose blood is this?"

"I can taste that bloody awful fungus that's growing everywhere!"

Leo stood aside as I tried to wipe Clive's face. He now seemed more willing to allow me to help. The water in the bowl was dark grey and clumps of muck floated on the surface. Luckily, all I could smell was lemon.

"Whose blood is this?" I repeated.

"That's just it," Clive said, "I don't know!"

As I wiped it from his face, I only succeeded in smearing it across his skin. This was not something I was used to. I looked at Leo.

He nodded. "I'll get the bathroom ready so you can have a shower. Some clean clothes, too."

Clive and I watched him leave the room.

Whatever was happening, I was starting to feel like it was spiralling out of my control – if I'd ever been in control in the first place.

The old man, who right now looked even older than his 80-odd years, whispered, "Janice spoke to me, Anne. She spoke to me."

"What has she been saying?" Having cleaned him up as best I could, I scrubbed my hands and dried them on a tea towel.

"That's just it, the more I think of it, the more I can't actually remember. It doesn't make any sense, and when I try to remember, it really bloody hurts my brain." As though to reinforce his words, he placed a hand to his forehead. His palm was pink with smeared blood. I had done a pretty useless job at cleaning him up.

"Tell me about all this blood, Clive," I said.

"I … I don't understand what's going on." His eyes flashed large and bright. A fleck of the black stuff clung to an eyelash. "Help me!"

I wondered how he came to be here, and assumed the pair must already be friends. Leo's house wasn't too far from our side of the village, just along the bridleway as I'd recently discovered.

"Did you walk over here?" I asked.

"Again," Clive whispered, "I don't remember."

I looked up from my nails that I hadn't realise I'd been picking. The varnish was embarrassingly chipped. "What do you mean?"

With a stronger voice, he said, "First I was on my sofa, watching ... watching ... TV ... I can't remember what I was watching." His gaze lingered towards a corner of the kitchen.

"Then what?"

"It was like the shadows just ..."

Somehow, I think I knew what he was about to add.

"... They just closed in on me. I don't know what happened then, but I found myself in the fields out back, near some rocks."

"Rocks?" I thought of what Leo had said about the shadows, and also the map of the world, and in particular the detailed map of Mabley Holt. The rocks were containment stones, Leo had said.

"I came to, covered in all this blood!" He held out his hands.

"Those stones are proving to be a large part of all this madness."

His shoulders slumped, and right at that moment the poor old man looked smaller than I'd ever known him to be. "Anne, whose blood is this?"

I opened a cupboard and pulled out two glasses. The light caught thumb prints and it made me question Leo's hygiene – I guessed he had a lot going on right now so who was I to pass judgement? I filled both glasses up with cold water and offered one to Clive. For a moment, he just stared at it. It was as though he didn't know what to do with it, so I placed it on the counter and sipped mine – deliberately slow so I no longer had to talk. The cold water chilled my throat, sharpening my senses. All I wanted was to head back home and sleep, and I had no idea of the time because the kitchen clock had stopped at 3:33.

When Leo returned, Clive quickly snatched up the glass. Water splashed his sleeve and spattered the floor. He gulped it, allowing some to dribble down his neck and soak his blood-stained jumper.

"Clive," Leo said, "come upstairs. You can clean yourself up here. I've left a towel and some clothes in the bathroom for you."

"Want me to come?" I asked.

Clive flashed a look of what could have been embarrassment, with eyes perhaps a little more focused. I guessed the cold water had stolen away his confusion.

"It's okay," Leo said, seeing the old man's look, "we can manage."

The two men left and I listened to their footsteps up the stairs and along the landing. I went back into Leo's study.

That damned painting.

What the hell was going on? I wanted to call the police, but knew there was so much more to come. Just as Leo had told me earlier, I doubted the police could do anything anyway. This was beyond anything I'd ever before experienced.

I glared at the canvas that sat crooked on the armchair. Leo claimed it was by a woman called Pippa, his neighbour for God's sake. Disregarding how incredible the whole thing was, I could not deny the woman's talent. The damn thing could stay there; I didn't want to touch it. I set about rummaging through the chaos that littered Leo's desk. I didn't give a shit if he cared about my invasion of his privacy.

That painting was an invasion of mine.

I flicked through the papers on the desk. Nothing made sense. The aged book titled *Necromeleons* was heavy and the page it fell open on was one that had been bookmarked by a receipt for bread and milk. The page depicted a black and white sketch of a jagged outcrop of rock covered with interesting symbols. And it was no surprise that those symbols were precisely like those I'd seen in the river. Another sketch was of a row of stone fragments set out in a circle on a grassy hill. It reminded me of Stonehenge. The text was a mix of German and French. Perhaps even Latin. I had no idea; numbers had always been my thing. A flick through the book showed more chunks of text and peculiar sketches of demons and devils and dark patterns that I could only describe as twists of shadow. Which, given all that had been explained, came as no surprise. I placed the book back down.

Poking out from under a bunch of photocopied notes on witchcraft and demonology and stone etchings, an aged Polaroid snatched my curiosity. It was a close-up of one of the symbols. Just like one I'd seen in the river: two triangles with facing apexes, one hollow and the other solid, separated by a crudely shaped X.

What did this mean? It seemed to be stamped or marked everywhere. Even on the spine of that large book.

Dropping the Polaroid back on the desk, I went to the large map on the wall, in particular to the one of the British Isles and the detailed map of Mabley Holt and the surrounding area. Various coloured pins dotted around it. There were about a dozen, some quite close, others a little further in the fields. One red pin marked the river that I'd fallen into. Again I wasn't surprised. Thinking of that embarrassing moment, I wondered whether I could still in fact taste the water.

Such was my concentration I didn't notice Leo had entered the study until he came to stand by my side.

"I …" I began, but couldn't say anything else.

He laughed and simply said, "Yeah, I know."

Apparently, Clive hadn't said much to Leo upstairs and still didn't reveal whose blood had covered him. When I'd suggested calling an ambulance, Leo had again been firm just as he had when I'd mentioned the police. We then spoke about the artist, Pippa, and he assured me I'd meet her the following day.

The aroma of coffee filled the kitchen where we were both now leaning against the counter, each with a steaming mug in hand.

"Tell me," I said, "about the Shadow Fabric."

Leo scratched his stubble. "As I mentioned earlier, the Shadow Fabric is a sentient darkness, existing inside the veil between this world and another."

I gestured with my mug for him to continue.

"Although the Fabric predates the 17th century, it was about that time all over the globe when the practice of witchcraft threw it into overdrive. It was stitched into such a concentration of evil that it's been a real pain in the arse ever since ..."

I waited for him to continue but he squinted into his mug.

"What do you mean by stitched?"

"Good question." The look on his face: was that sadness?

"Also, why is the Cat's mouth stitched up?"

"Without going into details of the apparatus used, I can tell you that stitching is pretty much what it suggests, only without the use of a needle and thread." He sipped his coffee. "There was ... is ... a particular technique in witchcraft that can harness evil and when linked, strengthens the Fabric. Stitched, you see?"

"I think so."

"The stitches that weave the Cat's mouth closed are no doubt threads of Fabric."

"It's all about the Shadow Fabric."

A brief smile cracked his face. "Last year, I managed to banish it beyond the veil. With help. It wasn't just me." He took another sip and rested an elbow on the kitchen counter.

"How has it returned?"

"It seems to be only traces of the Shadow Fabric this time. We won. But from what I can tell, it's returned on a different level. It seems to be a conduit."

"To allow the entities to get through?"

"Yeah." He grinned. "Precisely."

Given all that had occurred so far, I accepted what he just told me. Twenty-four hours ago I wouldn't have, but it was like I now trod a different path and I knew for certain I could not view life how I used to. For me, a whole new understanding of our existence had just been unveiled.

As we drank our coffees in silence, Clive came into the kitchen. The old man wore a pair of Leo's grey combats and a baggy green hoodie. Strange to see him in something else other than a yellow jumper, yet still he looked frail and confused. The poor man.

"I'm so tired," he said. "I want to go home."

"You can sleep here if you want," Leo offered.

I looked at the clock and remembered it was broken. Whatever the time, I guessed it was late.

"Kind of you, thank you." Clive eyed my mug as I placed it down on the counter.

"You want a coffee?" Leo asked him. "Tea?"

"No." Clive rubbed his hands together as though blood still covered them. "Thank you."

"Do you feel any better?" I asked. Although fresh from the shower, his eyes remained small and troubled.

"I'd like to go home now, please," he said without looking at me.

"Of course," I said. "I'll take you."

"Will you guys be okay?" Leo asked.

"We'll be fine," said the independent woman inside me. "I need sleep." I suddenly realised how tired I was.

"I have some things to sort out tonight." Leo clutched his empty mug. "There's a lot I need to make sense of."

"And I'll be meeting this Pippa tomorrow, too," I told him, hoping this man would be good to his word.

"You will," he replied, "no worries."

Clive and I saw ourselves out as Leo returned to his study.

A sharp blue moonlight pressed down on us as we stepped outside, and Clive quietly shuffled alongside me. There was much I wanted to ask him, but I guessed he'd had about as much of this as I had. I wanted to go home too, but I knew sleep was far away; what with the evening's excitement and having just drank coffee, I'd be alert for a while yet.

Luckily the moon lit our way through the canopy of branches over the bridleway, seeing as we were without a torch. With every step, I desperately wanted to ask Clive more about the ghost of his wife, but I felt a little awkward. I still wondered where all that blood came from. Eventually I followed Clive along his path and towards the front porch. As we stopped, I again thought of how strange it was to see him without his yellow jumper.

"Are you going to be okay?" I didn't want to leave him. "You want me to come in?"

"I just want to sleep," he said and avoided my eyes. "Thank you."

"I should come in," I insisted. This poor man had been covered in blood and filth, and I was convinced that there'd be evidence inside his house.

He shook his head. "Please, I just want to sleep."

I watched him shuffle through the porch, almost tripping over his own feet. Evidently both doors had been left unlocked. It was lucky we lived in an area where we didn't have to worry about burglaries. He disappeared inside without looking back. I imagined him walking into his lounge, those curtains still drawn, and him immediately calling for Janice.

For several moments I considered following him inside, just to make sure he was okay, then thought better of it. Back out on the road I gave a casual look across the fields and almost willed the Black Cat to be there; I saw nothing.

I needed to go home. Now. Further along the lane, the silvery haze of fog beneath moonlight drifted across the tarmac.

Then I did see something. Or some*one*. A silhouette, an ambling shadow. It was Harriet, her slightly rotund frame unmistakable. What was it with my neighbours? All I wanted was to go indoors.

I again wondered if I should phone the police.

Her silhouette shrank into the distance, vanishing into the thickening fog. Half of me wanted to go home, lock the door behind me and wait for all this insanity to pass. But I knew I couldn't, and it wouldn't. Whatever was happening in the Holt, I had somehow become part of it.

So, I jogged along the lane to reach where I last saw my neighbour. My *other* neighbour.

"Seriously?" I whispered.

What was going on with everyone?

I reached the corner of an adjacent lane that wound off towards another section of village.

Still no Harriet.

What I did see was the roadside rescue truck and the towed red van. Still attached, they were parked up in a passing place that was more an unofficial arc of crumbled tarmac and thick mud. The passenger's door of the truck gaped wide and pressed against the bushes.

I slowed my pace and reached the truck.

The front wheel had sunk into the mud and the driver's door hadn't been closed properly. Even though I didn't want to, my hand went for the handle. It was cold and wet with the moist atmosphere. I pulled – heavier than it should've been but I guessed it was due to the vehicle's angle. It creaked as I swung it wide.

The smell of cigarette smoke and energy drinks wafted out at me.

No sign of the men, and the key was still in the ignition. Maybe they had both got out after the truck broke down. A breakdown truck breaking down; there was something amusing in that but I couldn't even smile. Why leave it with the doors open and the key still inside?

Weird enough for the truck to be left like this … and then I saw the seat belts. They snaked across the seats, shredded. I wasn't surprised to see streaks of the black fungus – or *residue*, as Leo had explained – all over the upholstery and dashboard. No evidence of anything else, not even a struggle. Who could do this? More to the point, *what* could do this?

I stepped back and my foot landed awkwardly in a pothole. I looked down. For a moment, the moon hid behind heavy cloud, dropping an almost suffocating darkness over me. It only lasted a second or two, although long enough to make me freeze. Moonlight again washed over me. Relief. Across the tarmac, streaks of glistening mud led away from the vehicle. All I could think was they had to be drag marks from both truck driver and van driver.

The marks ended in the middle of the road, so I couldn't tell which direction they'd been taken in – if indeed they had been taken. This was crazy. Maybe … maybe what? They'd gone for a midnight stroll? Perhaps the Cat had dragged the bodies through the small hole in the bushes that led into the fields. Towards the river.

I walked to the centre of the road. Had it been the Cat that had dragged them out? Both men together? I guessed they were unconscious.

All these questions were doing my head in. Within five strides, I made it to the gap in the bushes to look across the field.

Harriet stood motionless halfway between the road and the woodland that led down to the river.

No sign of the men's bodies.

Fog and shadow drifted towards Harriet, seeming to pump from the ground. Her arms hung, and it looked as though small whirlwinds of mud and mist coiled around her wrists.

And like a tornado, the darkness knotted together and circled her, the fog churning with it. Thicker and faster, obscuring my view. A howling wind spat debris in the air. My breath snatched in my throat as I felt that wind cold against my face. I squinted into it, mesmerised.

No more than two seconds passed and that black hurricane collapsed. It simply slumped, like a magic act where the magician's cloth first hid the assistant and then didn't, just flattened to the stage as though no one was there in the first instance. Harriet was gone.

A final blast of wind pushed hair in my face, while my heartbeat seemed to pulse in my head.

The moon spotlighted an empty field.

I returned to my house for a scarf and gloves. As I pushed open my front door, it hit something on the mat and stopped dead. After an awkward manoeuvre, I bent to pick up whatever it was.

A rolled-up canvas.

For a second or two, I stared at it. No guesses as to who the artist could be but why would the woman, whom I'd not even met, remove the wooden frame and post it through my letter box? Given that I'd been out pretty much all day, I also wondered how long it had been there.

I unravelled it and for a moment didn't understand. The artwork was of something so simple. Much simpler than the other I'd found at Leo's.

It turned my stomach.

This painting depicted a faded and threadbare rug near a dark wooden bed leg. Simple, certainly, but it was what those familiar vivid strokes of turquoise revealed that got me.

I recognised it.

It was of my grandparents' bedroom floor. Their rug, to be precise. From the time I'd dropped Gran's turquoise nail varnish and it stained the fibres.

"What are you playing at?" I screamed at the woman who wouldn't be able to hear me. My heart seemed to rise and fill my throat.

In seconds, I was up the stairs and across the landing, the canvas screwed up in a fist. There I stood, before my grandparents' bedroom door that I'd not opened since I'd hidden away their urns. Five months; such a long time.

My hand hovered in front of me.

With a ridiculous amount of effort, my fingers curled around the cold handle. I twisted it and pushed the door wide. A musty smell wafted out at me. Dark blue moonlight pressed through the net curtains, creating silhouettes of the tall wardrobe and the bed, and also the bedside cabinets and a chest of drawers in the corner.

Two ceramic urns sat on the chest. One red, one blue. Gran. Grandad.

I stepped into the room and the smell of *them* tugged at memories. Gran. Grandad.

I switched on the light and squinted.

The furniture looked precisely the same, although now covered with a haze of dust. The flowery bedspread, smoothed out with crisp precision, reminded me of the time I'd gone shopping with Gran. We'd bought it on a trip to Hastings.

My gaze kept floating towards the urns.

The canvas flopped against my leg as I approached the bed. I didn't want to go around to Gran's side, knowing that turquoise stain would be there. But why had Leo's neighbour painted it, and then posted the stupid thing to me?

Beside the two urns sat Gran's jewellery box, embroidered and lined with sequins that once glinted. Now, however, beneath a layer of dust the fabric and sequins were dull and lifeless like my grandparents' ashes. As a child, I used to marvel at how large the box was, yet now, alongside the urns, it looked too small to contain all the treasures I once admired. Gran had always loved it when I made a fuss of her jewellery; I remembered as a girl I'd rummage through rings and bracelets, earrings and necklaces. Old, tarnished, I'd never cared. Nor had I cared that those rings never fit my tiny fingers, or that my ears weren't pierced, or how the bracelets would never remain on my thin wrists.

Without realising, I'd walked round the room to stand in reaching distance of the jewellery box … and my grandparents' ashes.

At my feet, and although faint, the turquoise stain dredged up the memory of Gran's shriek after I spilt the varnish. At the time, it seemed I cried for hours; I'd only wanted to be like her with those pretty fingers, I wanted to be an adult.

Now? I no longer wanted to be an adult; I'd had enough. All I wanted was to be that innocent little girl again, way back when life was easier. Much easier.

My legs folded and I slumped on the edge of the bed. I threw the canvas beside me and sank my head into clammy palms. I felt suffocated, like the ceiling wanted to collapse. Squeezing my eyes closed, I imagined the dark attic above with its cobwebbed rafters ... and beyond that, the roof tiles and chimney stack and the thick fog that smothered the house, the village, the world. My world.

No tears. Yet my heart thumped behind tight lungs.

The mattress moved, sank. Like someone—

I pressed my fingertips into my forehead, not wanting to budge, not wanting to look.

It was like someone was sitting at the bottom of the bed.

Just like when I was a child, when Gran or Grandad came into my room to sit on the bed, I felt the mattress tilt beneath their weight.

It was absurd, I had to snap out of this. I was upset and imagining things. I straightened my back, opened my eyes.

Of course, no one was there ... But ...

An imprint on that once-smooth bedspread slowly rose, settled, and returned to how it had been.

I leapt up, the canvas falling to the floor, and I threw my gaze around the room. Nothing, no one.

No ghosts.

If Janice's ghost floated around inside Clive's house, who was to say either of my Grandparents' ghosts didn't wander around here, too? I honestly did not know how to feel about that. It was all insane.

Totally. Insane.

I stood there, listening to my breath, just daring something else to happen. Still nothing ... Eventually, I crouched to pick up the canvas. It had fallen beside the stained corner of the rug where a tiny triangle of white paper hid beneath the flattened tassels.

With a fingertip, I slid it free in a curl of grit and dust.

A photograph.

My grandparents, not looking any different to how I remembered them, smiled back at me from beside a rock that jutted from the woodland floor. The churned mud at its base was disturbed like I'd seen earlier, as though it had pushed up from the ground. Grandad had an arm around Gran while she pressed one hand against the rock. Red and yellow paint covered the surface in places, the same bold curves and lines I'd seen beneath the river. Janice leaned against the other side of the rock, her arms folded. The back of her head rested against it. They all wore big coats and muddy hiking boots. I guessed Clive was behind the lens.

When I finally got to my feet, straightening up and still clutching the photo, I saw that the covers weren't even wrinkled. Not even from where I had sat a moment ago.

A chill crawled up my spine and clutched at my scalp.

It was all I could do to keep my hand from shaking as I stared at the photograph. I brought it up closer to my face. The markings on the stone looked sharper where Gran's hand was, almost as though they glowed. Perhaps it was nothing, just the sunlight from somewhere overhead, spearing down through the branches.

My fist pummelled Leo's front door as my heart raced with my breathing. I'd run all the way from my house to his, making a promise to get my lazy arse to the gym once all this crazy shit had passed – if indeed it would ever pass. The shadows in the overgrown bushes made me think of the way that whirlwind had swept away Harriet.

I banged the door again and rang the bell.

No answer.

Where was he? I thumped on the wooden panel again, this time hurting my hand. My breath plumed towards the moon as I stepped back to look up at a window.

"Leo?" I called in that loud whisper-hiss that wasn't a whisper at all. I'd not been gone long, surely he couldn't be asleep already. He'd said he had stuff to do.

From my left, in the front garden adjacent to his, I heard footsteps. For a moment, I thought of the Black Cat.

"Anne?"

I stumbled on the loose paving as I turned. Leo's face appeared between overgrown bushes and a broken wooden trellis.

"What are you doing over there?" I demanded, not meaning to shout at him.

His smile wasn't reassuring. "Come round, I have someone you need to meet."

"Who?" I stupidly asked, thinking only of the photograph and the madness I'd witnessed in the field. "Why?"

He stepped away from the bushes where I assumed he returned to his neighbour's front door. I went back out onto the road, and he watched me skirt the bushes and head up the path towards him. It was more unkempt than his front garden. I stepped over a trailing vine that had pushed out from the undergrowth. Its slick skin sported a row of vicious-looking barbs.

"You okay?" he asked when I stood beside him.

I shook my head. My mouth opened but the words froze on my lips.

"Anne?"

"The …" I said without knowing where to begin. "I saw the fog and shadows take Harriet in some kind of miniature hurricane. It snapped her up and she vanished. And I found the roadside rescue truck. The men weren't in there. And …" I swallowed, realising I was babbling. "And now I've found a photo that shows my Grandparents with Clive and Janice around a rock."

Leo nodded. "This is getting worse." He had his woolly hat bunched high on his head as he rubbed his forehead. He looked about as worn down as I felt.

I tried to say more but couldn't.

"I have a massive headache," he said. He pulled the hat down and did a bad job of straightening it.

We both turned to face the front door. He rapped knuckles on the wood as he slid a key into the lock. "Pippa," he called and twisted the key, "I'm here with a friend."

It was strange that he should let himself in with a key, which made me think perhaps the two were seeing each other. We stepped into the house. None of the lounge lights were on, although from a back room a faint yellow glow reached out at us.

Entering this house, owned by a woman who'd painted both me scrambling from the river and a stained rug from a childhood accident, was peculiar for too many reasons. I could not believe I was even entertaining the idea, but I guessed she was some kind of medium or clairvoyant. I didn't know the difference or if they were indeed the same because up until that moment, I'd never even considered the possibility of any of it.

The smell of paint didn't come as a surprise, yet underneath that was a whiff of dog. Not unpleasant though, just that animal musk. As we neared the back room, a golden retriever ambled towards us.

Leo crouched and vigorously rubbed the dog's head.

"Georgie," he said, "how the devil are you?"

I looked beyond them and into a room that seemed to be covered wall to wall with canvasses.

"Pippa," Leo said and stood up, "this is Anne."

In the corner of the room with her back to us, a woman sat before a large easel. Several smaller ones arced around the room behind this and obscured the window and a surrounding wall that looked like it had recently been repaired.

"Hello, Anne." Her voice was small. Her dark hair was pulled back in a messy pony tail. She swiftly pulled up her hood, and still faced away from us.

"Hi," I answered, feeling incredibly tiny among all the amazing artwork. Most were acrylic paintings, with several pencil sketches strewn about the floor and pinned between larger pieces. Many paintings were typically colourful landscapes, similar to those that surrounded Mabley Holt. I recognised the local church and its steeple. In contrast, there were several where it looked like people had been crucified and even burned at the stake. Grim. Her talent was such that her brush strokes depicted motion; the rushing water beneath a bridge, the swaying body hanged from a branch, the roar of flames.

All gruesome stuff.

"We're trying to find the centre of all this weird shit," Leo explained.

I wanted to demand why this woman had painted things she couldn't possibly know, but instead I muttered, "It's nice to finally meet you."

"It's a pleas—" Pippa began, but then she jerked upright. Grabbed one of her brushes and leaned in towards the easel to continue painting.

"She often does that," Leo said to me.

I watched the young woman make frantic sweeps with the brush. Browns and green slapped across the canvas. Flecks of paint peppered the floor and her clothes. She dabbed her brush in a chipped mug that brimmed with black paint, and began dotting the landscape with it, darkening particular areas. I wondered if all artists used mugs for painting. My eyes kept drifting back towards the woman burning at the stake. That pained look on her face. A witch, I had no doubt.

I didn't know what to say.

Half-hidden behind a cloth streaked with rainbow colours, one canvas revealed an impressive black cat, its flank glistening beneath moonlight. The eyes burned red above a stitched mouth. One side of its head was bald, scarred.

"The Black Cat of the Holt," I said. Grandad had seen it and so had I.

Pippa's frantic brushstrokes created an outline of a truck. With all that I'd so far witnessed, I was not surprised.

"I've just found that," I whispered to Leo, "just up the road."

In addition to what I'd already discovered, Pippa added the next piece to the mystery. We watched in silence as the story unfolded. For a full ten minutes, maybe longer, I dared not budge.

She used whites and greys to paint the shimmering form of a spirit half in, half out of the cab. Folds of shadow traced its limbs. The bulk of the roadside rescue driver hid the spirit's head as it dragged the unconscious man from the cab.

Pippa went about putting the finishing touches to the painting, where it explained the disappearance of the other man, the man with whom I'd briefly spoken. A vortex of darkness churned in the bottom corner of the canvas. Again, such was Pippa's talent of depicted motion, I saw how the shadows – this was the Shadow Fabric – rippled and churned, warping reality.

All that remained of the van driver was his screaming face.

I assumed the roadside rescue man had followed soon after, luckily unconscious.

During the time I watched this story unfold, I'd undone my coat. My scalp itched and I felt as though a headache was fast approaching; the paint fumes, stress, terror; the combination of all this shit.

I needed some fresh air.

Finally, Pippa dropped her brush to the floorboards and it bounced in a black splash. She reached to the side and picked up a pair of dark glasses I'd not noticed. Standing, she put them on and adjusted her hoodie.

She turned.

The only part of her face I could see was her nose. The sunglasses hid her eyes, a scarf hid her mouth and cheeks, and the hoodie covered the rest of her head. Perhaps she was scarred. Like the Cat.

"The men have been taken through the Fabric," she said. This time her voice was stronger, clearer. Muffled though, behind the scarf. "For the Construct."

I was about to ask what she meant, when Leo interrupted.

"A demon is building a construct?"

"Yes," Pippa answered him.

"It's using the flesh of those men," Leo explained, seeing my expression, "to build a vessel to walk the earth again."

"Th—" My tongue failed me. I swallowed. "Those poor men." I looked at another painting. This one was of what looked like a witch burning on a pyre while the villagers looked on. "I'm not exactly sure how much more I can handle."

"I understand," Pippa said, "I was once innocent to all this chaos, then I seemed to get sucked in. Those Black Cat sightings have been going on for years, centuries in fact, but you already know that. It's all part of the picture."

"What is going on?" I asked. "I don't understand any of this. How have you painted things you couldn't possibly know?"

She stepped forward and I flinched ... She came up short, standing before me in the centre of the room. At her feet, Georgie nestled against her leg.

"Your neighbour," she said. "He's in danger."

Looking at this woman, the way her paint-smeared cardigan hung from frail shoulders, I guessed she was in her forties. Even though I couldn't see her eyes, the skin of her nose looked young. I wondered if she was closer to thirty years old.

Leo looked from me to the woman. "No time for a cup of tea then, Pip?"

"No," she whispered.

I scanned the paintings once again. As I opened my mouth to ask about the one she'd painted of me falling into the river, she grabbed hold of both our arms. Her fingers dug in.

"You must go," she said, her voice low. "Now!"

I stood behind Leo as he entered Clive's porch to hammer on the inside door. After leaving Pippa's studio, we had rushed to my neighbour's house, the artist's urgent words chasing us through the night. Leo knocked again, and rang the doorbell.

I didn't expect an answer. There were no footsteps from inside, nothing. As I listened to the silence, I wondered about Harriet and how I'd seen a shadowy whirlwind steal her away.

Not giving my elderly neighbour enough time to even get to the door, Leo tried the handle. It turned, and he glanced at me. I shrugged, unsurprised that it was open. I had, after all, done the same the previous night … which seemed such a long time ago.

We entered Clive's house.

The first thing that hit me was the smell of the sea with an underlying stink of something like overcooked vegetables. It reminded me of a visit to one of Gran's friends when I was younger, who lived in a warden-controlled block of flats. I remembered how the long walk down the hallway always reeked of a multitude of dinners.

Several lampshades forced back shadows. Again, I thought of the way the shadows had taken Harriet. I hoped the shadows here were harmless. Similar to the previous night when I'd entered alone, moonlight leaked around the curtains. I expected to see him in his chair, but it was empty.

"Clive?" Leo called, his voice startling me. My thoughts had begun to drift towards the possibility of seeing Janice's ghost again.

"Clive," Leo called again, "are you in here?"

Floorboards creaked beneath each footfall as we made our way through the lounge. Nothing had changed much since I was last in his home.

From upstairs, something thumped. Loud.

Leo and I froze.

The light fitting swayed. Another two thumps echoed down to us, but not as loud as the first. With Leo in the lead, we charged for the stairs, and in seconds we were on the landing. That heavy stink was even stronger.

"Clive?" I shouted and slapped the light switch. The brightness made me squint.

Something moved in the room at the far end of the hall.

Leo had his head round the nearest doorframe as I barged past him, heading for the end of the landing. I shoved the door wide. About to call Clive's name again, I halted on the threshold. Gloom filled what once had perhaps served as a guest room. A white haze of fog pushed against the window beside a single bed, barely illuminating anything. An unremarkable chest of drawers sat beside it. In the other corner was—

I inhaled the foul, cold air.

At first, I could not make out what I looked at. I did not want to turn on the light; the light from behind me was enough to allow me to see.

Bloody handprints covered the walls and the rumpled bedspread. But it was not that which turned my stomach.

"Jesus Christ." Bile rose in my throat.

Splayed over two walls and part of the ceiling, framed by peeled and blackened wallpaper, a sheet of tangled limbs quivered. Shredded clothes, darkened by what I assumed was blood, seemed stitched with glistening skin that was impossibly stretched in places between patches of hair. The greasy stitches that wove through the chunks of flesh looked like those that held the Black Cat's lips closed.

A chill crawled up my spine as I spotted several hairy nipples, again too far from one another. Jagged splinters of ribcage and other bones stuck at odd angles from the skin, their ends dripping that familiar black filth.

I felt Leo's breath on my neck as he peered over my shoulder. Although his mouth was close to my ear, his voice sounded miles away as he said, "What the fuck?"

More to myself than to him, I said: "Where are their heads?" Again, bile rose in my throat. Somehow, I managed to swallow it down, the bitterness snatching me from my daze. In the space of twenty-four hours – had it been that long? – I had seen the Black Cat for myself, a ghost, and now this Frankenstein horror.

The woven skin and bone, of jean material and T-shirt and shirts, was like a patchwork quilt. But it was the stitches, they … they somehow twitched as though with a life of their own. I remembered how Leo had mentioned the darkness was sentient, a veil between worlds, he'd said. Those stitches were indeed a part of the Shadow Fabric. If I'd ever needed proof, then here it was.

On the floor below this nightmare, a heap of crimson muck had soaked into the carpet. What I assumed had been the thumps we'd heard were fleshy sacks of muscle and offal that quivered amid barbed vines – similar to the one I'd stepped over in Pippa's garden. The vines snaked and twitched, flexing upwards as though trying to reach for the appendages above.

"Leo …" I whispered.

He squeezed past me, into the room. I had no desire to get any closer and so stepped back. Even so, I glimpsed a tattoo on what I guessed had once been a man's arm.

"It's the van driver." I recognised it from when the man had waved towards where he'd spotted the Black Cat.

Faint wisps of what looked like tendrils of smoke coiled around the stitched parts, weaving in and out of the flesh. Yellow pus oozed, trickling down the swollen lumps.

I clamped my mouth so tight my jaw ached.

"This is not good," Leo mumbled.

"You're not kidding!" I wanted to hit him for his understatement. A familiar feeling of tightening lungs took hold, but I refused to give in to any hysteria.

Some of the stitches twitched and curled like beckoning fingers, trying to reconnect to the ragged flesh above. Absurdly they reminded me of a baby's tiny hand reaching for its mother, desperate to clamp those little digits around a finger.

Leo took a step forward.

"What are you doing?" For the first time since meeting this man, I wondered if I could even trust him. Perhaps he was behind it all.

I backed up, watching as he advanced on the thing. Now out in the hallway, I got ready to turn and run. But out of the corner of my eye, something moved. Something in between me and the top of the stairs. The shadows parted.

There stood Janice.

My dead neighbour's incorporeal form shimmered, little more than a smudge against a backdrop of the landing, the bannister and balustrades.

Every inch of my skin cooled and I felt my jaw slacken. I turned on legs that threatened to trip me, and I grabbed at the door frame, almost missing it. My hand slid in fungus. Repulsed, I lurched away to find myself beside Leo in the centre of the room.

Out in the hall, the image of Janice slid in and out of focus, faint spirals of fog and shadow blended with her hazy form.

Leo yelled.

I turned.

Black tendrils of solid shadow had looped around his wrist, blistering the skin. His sleeve had ridden high up his forearm as he wrestled with it. The stink of burning flesh filled the room. He had a tattoo of that familiar symbol I'd seen on both the rocks and the *Necromeleons* book. Quick thoughts fired through my brain as I lunged to help: although the symbol looked more like a scar, it could've even been from an old burn. For the first time, I saw the shape comparable to an hourglass.

"Anne!" Leo shouted through his agony. "Get out!"

Behind him, the room darkened.

A blend of fog and shadow leaked from the seething mass of glistening flesh and bone. Was this the Fabric? Whatever it was, it had taken over the room, obscuring the bedroom furniture. As that darkness wrapped around more of his body and arm, he managed to snatch something from his boot. A knife?

In a tornado of darkness, he was gone.

"Leo!" I yelled.

I grabbed at the door frame again, only this time held on tight, caring little for the sticky shit that oozed between my fingers. One second he'd been there and the next, he wasn't; he'd vanished into the draping void behind him.

In the corner, the stitched monstrosity of those two headless bodies writhed in a torrent of black waves. Between that Frankenstein monster and me, glinting in the strange light of the room, was Leo's knife. More an ornamental knife, like a sacrificial dagger that belonged in those Hammer Horror movies Grandad loved.

A darkness spread up the wall, seeming to ooze from the plaster itself. It splayed outwards behind the abomination like creeping damp spores, further darkening the room. With one last thrash of wobbling, pus-slick limbs, its entire fleshy body slid backwards to sink into the dark mass.

It was as though the wall wasn't even there.

In a cacophony of slurps and crackles and squelches, the stitched lump of fat flesh that had once been two men, disappeared into the void. And like filthy water sucked down a plughole, the darkness shrank, closing in, giving way once again to the wall. Black smears remained. And bloody handprints.

The knife remained on the floor among heaped red and black muck. Faint coils of fog teased the blade.

The knife. It was Leo's, but I suspected I needed it. I needed a weapon, certainly. I needed something; I felt so naked. With my boot, I nudged it free from the muck, then grabbed it. I turned and stumbled from the room.

I'd forgotten about the ghost of Janice.

Janice stood before me, blocking my retreat. She wore the dress I'd seen in Clive's photo, only her form was transparent. Like your everyday ghost, I saw straight through her: the balustrade behind, the outlines of the bedroom doors beyond, and the window at the end of the landing. Her face shimmered in coils of light, a faint luminescence amid twists of shadow.

I didn't know what was louder, my heartbeat or my breathing.

The ghost's lips parted, mist drifting across her face.

"Help me," she said, her mouth out of sync with her voice. It was like watching a badly dubbed movie.

My hand tightened around the knife.

Witch ...

I had no idea where that thought came from. Janice hadn't spoken. Instead it was like a tiny voice at the back of my mind. Was it telling me this phantom woman was, or had been, a witch? Is this anything to do with Pippa's impressive artwork?

Blade.

There it was again, that voice. The knife warmed in my grip, getting hotter, hotter ...

"You don't need that," Janice said. I assumed she meant the knife.

"I ..." I struggled to find words in a dry throat. "I'd rather keep it."

I was talking to a ghost, for bloody-hell's sake.

"Please," she said, a sadness pulling at her eyes. "Please find Clive, he's in danger."

"I don't know where he is."

My breath drifted through the apparition. Her transparent form wavered, swaying with her dress. Pools of shadow licked the carpet, the skirting, and traced her shoes that hovered above the floor.

"You know where he is," she assured me. "You've seen where it started."

"What?" I had no clue where she meant.

Her eyes glazed over and her eyelids flickered.

"You can save him, please."

"Where?"

Her eyes flitted left and right. "You must!"

I thought of the blackened copse I'd seen the day before. Perhaps that's where it had started.

"Yes."

I guessed this apparition could read my mind. Given all this insanity, who was to say she couldn't?

"Yes," she said again and I didn't know if she was repeating herself or confirming my suspicions.

I should be running from the house right now, but I had something to do. I had to find Clive. Plus, it seemed I now needed to help his dead wife – I could not believe I was even entertaining such a crazy idea. My grip tightened around the knife. Besides, where the hell was Leo? Was he okay? He had fallen into the Fabric that I assumed took Clive – also Harriet for that matter. And that *thing* followed them all. Was it too late for them? Were they each now stitched together like that Frankenstein monstrosity?

I glanced over my shoulder.

"Your friend," Janice said, "he is with Clive."

How did she even know this?

"Find Clive, you will find your friend."

It made about as much sense as any of this did.

The ghost's eyes closed. "I cannot do anything from here, it has to …" Threads of darkness stitched her eyelids together. "… has to be …" More stitches wove through her lips, and her last words were muffled. "… be you."

The hallway light behind her dimmed. Her ghostly form stretched, blending with the fading light. My perception of the hallway behind warped as her form swirled with the churning fog.

She vanished.

I stepped back, still gripping the blade. My hand was hot, and I guessed it was because I held it so tight.

Witchblade.

Again, that voice inside my head.

This ornate knife, the one I held … was called a Witchblade? Some of the artist's paintings depicted witches. Mabley Holt was proving to be more than a village with Black Cat sightings. Pippa had somehow foreseen my involvement. Perhaps I should go talk to her before I went on some crazy rescue mission armed with a sacrificial blade.

I ran.

With the knife pointed to the floor so as not to stab myself, I ran downstairs and left the house. The chill mist dampened my skin when I staggered down the path.

"What the fuck?" I shouted, my breath joining the mist. I didn't know whether I should visit Pippa or head for the fields and to that blackened copse. Or indeed to leave the village. Just run. Get the hell out of this … this Hell.

No time for the artist; I had to find Clive and Leo, and Harriet if it wasn't too late for her.

Guided by a silver moon, I ran through the fog and across the fields. To think, this past week I'd been looking for a missing cat.

The damp air filled my lungs, my breath now rasping. I had no idea what the time was. Mud clumped my boots, and it wasn't easy to run in them, even though I'd managed so far – I'd certainly have some blisters soon, if not already. Every inch of me was hot and sticky.

I thought of the mud and the grass and the fog, and the sweat freezing my forehead as I ran … and thought nothing of what I was doing or what kind of Hell might be waiting for me. Odd how things can flash through your adrenaline-fuelled-scared-to-death mind when you're running through a field in the middle of the night, holding a witch's knife.

Finally, there was the copse.

Despite the blue-grey darkness beneath the cold moonlight, it looked different to how it had appeared earlier. Curls of mist draped around the jagged trunks and splintered branches that littered the ground. The trunks were smaller now. Shards of rock, much the same as the ones in my grandparents' photograph, had erupted from the earth. Chunks of smaller rocks dotted the blackened ground. Shadows, too. Deep, dark. And sentient. In places, they churned with the broiling mist. Fungus had sprouted in places. Each with a quivering head, sweaty, in a tangle of what I assumed were vines. Those vines slithered as though they were still growing.

The closer I got, the darker the mud at my feet became.

Rocks speared the ground at all angles, having risen from beneath the field. This was not the result of an earthquake. I'd learnt these rocks were containment stones to mark a buried demon, and so if they'd risen of their own accord …

Why the fuck wasn't I running in the opposite direction? Was I really heading to this place armed with a little knife?

The rocks had split into layers that reminded me of slate – I had no idea what type of rock they were – and a number of surfaces revealed coloured pictograms. At their base, the shadows moved. But ... it was cats. Perhaps a dozen cats roamed the darkness between tufts of burnt grass.

I jogged a little faster even though my stomach churned with fear. Hope. Murphy. Please God, let me find my little buddy.

Where was Clive? Where was Leo?

Some cats prowled, others were curled up against the rocks, some walked casually, while others stood alert with ears back; all seemed to give every stone attention. They had to be the domestic cats missing from around the village. More than a dozen. How were they all here?

Murphy was there somewhere, I knew it.

I wanted to call for him, yet my words didn't come – realising it may not be a good idea to reveal my presence. I doubted I'd manage anything anyway, with my lungs on fire the way they were.

There was Harriet. She crouched beside a shard of jutting rock with hands buried in the earth. Piles of dirt and broken stone heaped around her. There were no cats nearby; it was as though they deliberately kept clear of her. She continued to move her hands as though she rummaged beneath the surface in search of something.

A mound of earth proved to be a good spot for me to calm myself and hide from – what, the cats? The shadows? I had no idea, but I didn't want to get too close. Not yet. I didn't know what the hell I was doing.

Harriet straightened up, her arms coming free of the dirt. Mud and black filth dripped from her fingers.

My hand tightened around the hilt of the blade; somehow comforting. I moved out again, keeping close to the ground, slowing my approach and equally trying to slow my breathing.

Her hands twitched. For a moment, I wondered if she was behind all this – could she be a witch? I knew in this age of mobile phones and space travel there were self-professed witches out there. The modern-day witch was so far removed from the 17th-century burn-at-the-stake witch hunts of that era, and that made me think of Pippa's painting of the burning woman. In today's society, we had mediums and such. I'd never believed in clairvoyance or tarot or any of that nonsense, but I guessed people could exercise witchcraft if they wanted to. It's not all about the goat-sacrificing witchcraft from that horror movie I'd seen once with Grandad. I assumed modern-day witchcraft was much more … civilised? At least, there were a lot of people out there who believed in it. Me? I'd been a non-believer up until about twenty-four hours ago.

Keeping low to the ground, I rustled through the tall grass and past another heap of earth and headed for a chunk of rock. This one sat in a trench, and it looked like it had somehow been propelled from the centre of the copse. Who's to say it hadn't done precisely that?

Huddled in the shadows, I peered around its bulk.

Harriet moved. Her arms and legs wobbled, her head flopping back, and the shadows swept her upwards. A spreading darkness webbed from the giant shards of stone. It reminded me of the vortex from Pippa's canvas, the one she'd painted of the two men being pulled into the shadows.

The remaining blackened tree trunks splintered amid snaps and cracks. It sounded like gunshots. Traces of fog twisted and churned with the darkness as Harriet's body hovered overhead. Her arms and legs stretched back as coiling tendrils of shadow strung her up against the rock.

Several of the prowling cats stopped, hackles raising, tails bristling. They watched Harriet as more wispy shadows slid around her limbs. Black filth dripped from her saturated clothes.

Still she rose higher.

All the cats now appeared as though they didn't want to – or indeed, *couldn't* – approach the shadows that rippled along the ground. Fungus heads had sprouted in places, and barbed vines slithered through the tall grass and heaped mud. It was like the cats lurked on the perimeter, unable to advance, being held back by the twisting vines.

Something moved in the shadows beyond the perimeter of rocks.

Leo.

He had Clive with him, lugging the older man along with an arm draped over his shoulder. Black filth covered them both. Leo staggered, struggling to remain upright. A cat darted from beneath his feet as he lurched past one of the rocks. He looked up and his eyes widened as he saw Harriet in the air, those shadows stretched from stone to stone. He jerked sideways, trying to get further away, dragging Clive with him.

I stood. Not wanting to, but I had to help. I looked past the men, making sure nothing was nearby. No cats or anything else for that matter. Especially no shadows around.

Still, I kept low as I hurried forward approaching the huge stones, but staying on the perimeter.

Harriet screamed; loud and shrill on the night.

The poor woman had finally regained consciousness. She wrestled with the shadows as they tightened around her. Like a corkscrew of darkness, the shadows speared her hands and wound through her flesh, shredding her clothes. Flaps of skin swung from glistening bone as the darkness burrowed into her muscle and stripped it away.

Leo had backed up, yet it looked like one of those vines had wrapped itself around Clive's ankle. They both fell to the ground, their clothes slick with mud and muck. Leo kicked out at the vines and in retaliation they whipped and flailed, thumping and slapping the ground. He was on his knees, his head swaying; he looked ready to collapse.

I ran towards them, almost tripping as I neared the last stone. A cat darted away.

By now, overhead in a writhing mess of blood and shadow, Harriet's body was nothing but ripped clothes and bone shards, wobbling flesh and torn organs. All the while the darkness roiled around the gruesome mess in a frenzy.

Stitching.

It was stitching it together, piece by piece, out of shape and awkwardly angled, defying human anatomy.

I had to look away.

"Leo!" I said, not wanting to shout, not wanting to bring attention to us. I came to crouch beside the two men.

Blood soaked Clive's trousers where the vine clamped his ankle, lacerating his flesh with dozens of barbs. The old man dribbled, mumbling.

Gripping the Witchblade tighter, I hacked at the vines. Black muck sprayed, covering my hand and arm. It stung. Slick and sticky, the knife slipped in my grip, yet I held on. The stink filled my throat and I choked as I stabbed and slashed. Finally, the vine tore apart, wet and sinewy like a gutted fish, and it slithered away, retreating into the thicket of grass and fungus.

Clive's eyes rolled back in his sockets, his head swaying.

"Stay with me," I told him, wiping my hand on my trouser leg.

Leo was on his hands and knees, coughing.

"You okay?" I asked.

His eyes were bloodshot, staring through a slick mask of filth. He nodded.

The roar overhead diminished and we both turned to watch the shadows open up beneath the churned crimson mess that was once Harriet.

A stitched limb speared up from the darkness. Fog and shadow dispersed. Another. And another. Four of them, clutching at the edges of the void to pull itself free. It was the Frankenstein monstrosity from earlier, somehow more refined, smoother, more agile though it jerked like some clambering insect. It was like a bloated sack of patchwork skin, stitched with clothes.

"The Construct," Leo said. "The Demon must be near."

That fleshy Construct, still headless, floated upwards as though swept along on a black sea. The rush of blood and muck that no longer was Harriet twisted in an insane tornado of fog and shadow, and spun around the Construct.

In a blur, they stitched together.

"We need to get the fuck out of here, Leo," I said. "Now!"

There was a rustle from behind.

I turned.

At the same time, the moon slid behind a stretch of cloud and the shadows pressed in on us. Normal shadows, I hoped. There, with its great paws out in front as though ready to pounce, stood the Black Cat. Although the darkness smothered me, smothered us, I saw its outline of bristling hair and those burning eyes. Its silhouette in the darkness was more formidable than the quivering hulk of flesh in the centre of the whirling mass of Shadow Fabric.

It growled behind its stitched lips.

Moonlight washed over us. Relief.

So far, this beast hadn't harmed me. But with the horrific scene that was unfolding in the burned-out copse, I didn't fancy my chances. Slowly, I got up while Leo struggled to lift Clive.

Dirt fell from my trousers as I straightened up.

I glanced over at the stitched monster that had now sharpened, became more *real*. The shadows had thinned, too. Leo had Clive up on his knees, and the two men straightened into an awkward standing position.

The Black Cat was no longer there.

I stepped back, glancing left and right. All that remained of its presence was singed grass and drifting smoke.

Further along on the edge of the copse, in a whirlwind of fog and shadow, of mud and debris, the Cat reappeared again. It paced back and forth as though it tested the perimeter. With purposeful strides, it headed back in our direction. Then stopped …

Its eyes flared, it hunched, ready to pounce.

I froze, and screamed.

It darted towards us.

"Anne!" Leo shouted, "duck!"

I dropped to my knees, my hands slapping mud as the Cat bounded through the grass. Its paws hammered the ground, its breath steaming, and its eyes trailing a fire that spiralled in its wake. As it neared us, I waited for the impact, but it leapt overhead at the last moment, straight for the Construct. Hot wind rushed over us amid the heavy stink of animal and burning.

By now, the shadows around the copse had dispersed and the wobbling mass spread itself out across the grass, clutching at the charred trunks of branches. Smoke rose from where the fleshy lump shifted its weight. Pus and ichor oozed from between the patchwork of stitches.

Tiny fires licked the branches.

The Cat slammed into the monster with a wet thump. Filth sprayed everywhere, splashing the ground. Flames hissed.

All of the domestic cats shot off in different directions, heading away. Apart from one. This cat's movements, the shape, the way the tail swiped left and right as it moved, was unmistakable. I had no doubt who it was.

I stood slowly.

It was Murphy.

And he headed towards me.

Clamped in his mouth was what I guessed to be a mouse, or even a rat. It was large, that was for certain. In no hurry, with the Cat and Construct wrestling behind him, he strolled towards me. The closer he got, the more I realised it wasn't a rodent he had clamped between his teeth.

My stomach hollowed.

In his mouth was a hand. A human hand, shrivelled, almost skeletal.

Murphy dropped it by my boot and looked up at me.

While the Black Cat and the monster writhed nearby amid heaps of earth, broken stones, and blackened branches, I watched Murphy dart off across the field. Smoke burned in my throat. The surrounding fires strengthened to cast an orange glow on the decayed hand. Repulsed, I staggered backwards. A ring on one of the fingers glinted, reflecting the flames.

"Whose is that?" Leo asked as he came up alongside me, still struggling to keep Clive upright.

My voice sounded far away as I said, "Gran." I remembered learning of how she'd suffered serious wounds in the accident, but how had her hand ended up here? Why hadn't Murphy stayed with me?

Tears blurred my vision.

The Black Cat wrestled with the quivering mass of flesh, its hair slick with filth. The thing's lumpy appendages flopped as it fought off the attack. Loud, wet slaps echoed. The Cat only had its claws for weapons because of its mouth stitched the way it was, but it easily sliced through the disgusting patchwork flesh.

Clive murmured something.

With a surprising bout of sudden strength, as though from a hidden reserve, the old man shoved Leo aside.

"What the—?" Caught off guard, Leo lost his grip.

The old man lurched away, running off on unsteady legs. He wasn't even stooping, nor did he seem aware of the blood still gushing from his ravaged ankle.

He'd seen Janice.

The ghost of his wife stood between the two great stones, layers of shadow raged around her like black flames.

Further away in heaps of glistening muck, the fleshy monster quivered, its faceless hulk sweaty and oozing filth between its stitched mass. The Black Cat stepped back, dragging chunks of flesh with it, sinew caught on its claws, stringy and steaming. Although in ragged clumps, its stitches torn and the patchwork flesh shredded, the monster expanded as though it breathed in.

Still the Black Cat paced backwards, its head low to the ground, as was its tail.

"Clive!" I shouted. "Don't!"

Ignoring me, he neared the apparition of his dead wife. She held out her arms, shadowy tendrils corkscrewing around her fingers. The stones that framed her glowed, and sputtering flames traced the symbols and sigils that covered their surface.

Janice and Clive embraced. There was a solidity to her; a proper embrace.

He smiled, laughed, his eyes shining.

The Cat now glanced around the copse as though seeking assistance. None of the domestic cats, including my Murphy, were nearby.

Janice's hands lengthened, darkening as more shadows wrapped around her. Clive had his eyes closed, his head buried in her hair. His shoulders jerked; the poor man was sobbing.

"Janice isn't a ghost," Leo said and snatched the Witchblade from my hand.

"What do you mean?"

"Look!"

Shadows surrounded the pair. Then Janice's eyes darkened, her face darkened, her whole body darkened. All the while behind them both, the fleshy monster expanded once again. Several stitches tore, pus and blood dribbling as the segments came apart.

"It's the Demon."

"What?"

More shadows flowed around the pair, churning up the mist at their feet.

"It never was Janice, the sneaky little demon fucker!" Leo shouted.

The great patchwork creature ripped open further, the stitches breaking off in wriggling clumps. They snaked away, playing with the surrounding shadows. The split along the creature's bulk widened to reveal a dizzying haze of blood and darkness. Cartilage and bone spun, grinding together. It buzzed, muted by the fat flesh around it.

Time ... began ... to drag ...

Janice wrapped long arms around Clive, and in a blur of fog and shadow, hurled them both into the monster's grinding jaws. They tumbled into the gnashing bones and razor-edged cartilage, mashing them together. Janice's form swirled amid the bloody mess as Clive vanished in red and black whorls.

Leo stepped forward holding out the Witchblade. I had no idea what he intended. It was like I was watching everything in painstakingly slow motion.

Even the churning mess of Clive's body had slowed and I saw it all in grisly detail. His clothes and skin and bone shredded in a haze of crimson. It spattered across the ground, spewing over the patchwork flesh and dangling stitches. The spinning cartilage and bone ground his body down, like a millstone grinding a punnet of strawberries…

Slowly, round and round, it mashed his body into a pulp.

Still Leo gradually advanced. At his feet, fungus puffed tiny black clouds, and several vines crept towards him. Their barbs clicked as they slithered against small rocks.

My voice was equally slow as I called out to him: "Leeee-ooooo!" Those two syllables echoed, somehow muted.

There was a warmth in my palm and …

I looked down.

I held Gran's severed and shrivelled hand.

How …?

From the ragged stump of flesh where the wrist ended, faint swirls of white and blue entwined with the shimmering outline of a forearm, then a whole arm, then an entire—

In a long dragged out echo, I said, "Grrrraaaan?"

She stood beside me, holding my hand.

Gran.

Her ghost.

She wore khaki trousers and that big coat she'd favoured when hiking – precisely the same clothes she wore in the photograph where she had one hand on the rock.

In the corner of my eye, Leo had almost reached the grinding mess of Clive inside that spinning mouth. Tiny crackles of white energy spat from the Witchblade. A faint whiff of ozone drifted towards me.

Time slowed even more …

Gran.

Could this be a demon like Janice was? Could this also be a trick?

Her hand twitched. The shrivelled flesh lightened and smoothed out, became pink and wrinkled just as Gran's hand had once been. Her fingers curled around my own, and she squeezed. Tight.

Words failed me as I looked into the eyes of my dead grandmother.

She smiled.

And then darkness pulsed with each squeeze of the hand. It lowered, embracing me. Coming down, dropping like a blanket – like *fabric* – now faster than everything else. It came at me in waves, in a flood of gloom, of strangling blackness. But this was soothing … I again wondered for a moment if the whole thing was some demon trickery, just as Clive had been fooled.

Gran turned our hands over to reveal faint traceries of white and yellow energy spitting between our hands. It was similar to what I'd just seen emitting from the Witchblade. She gently released me … a lingering touch remaining as energy spat across our knuckles, transferring a row of symbols and sigils from her palm onto mine.

The warmth enveloped me, and with a sensation like pins and needles it spread up my arm, encasing my entire being.

Electrifying.

Powerful.

From deep within my gut, a growl shook my consciousness alert. Deep, shuddering, it was like an engine. It took over everything, filled my body, shaking me. Still I felt the tingle of electricity as though charged by the energy Gran had transferred.

Darkness. I couldn't open my eyes.

Was Gran still with me?

I tried to call out for her but my lips were closed. They failed to open and for a moment, panic flushed through me. What was going on? Light from somewhere. Faint. Finally, I managed to open my eyes. Darkness gave way to an orange flickering light. I was still in the copse, surrounded by burning stones and blackened trees. There was Leo, he crouched by the side of—

My body.

Away from where I stood, I lay on the ground, eyes closed. Leo held the Witchblade in one hand, while he searched my neck for a pulse with the other.

Was I dead?

Was I having an out of body experience?

Still I couldn't open my mouth. I wanted to call for him. My legs moved of their own volition. Only … only I had four legs. I gazed about the copse, looking between the upright stones and splintered tree trunks. Fires licked and raged around me.

I strolled forwards. Again, without wanting to. My legs … Four legs … My tail stiffened.

I was the Cat. The Black Cat.

No longer Guardian, I was now Saviour. I had to end this Daemon here on Earth.

I advanced with an energy that fired through my veins, pulsing and raging through me. I bounded towards the Daemon – the Daemon that was in its final level of Construction.

As my paws thumped the mud and filth that covered the ground, I understood. As fucking crazy as this was, there was I, little Anne of the Holt, finally understanding everything: the Daemon, long since trapped beneath and between the Sigil Stones, had manipulated a Mortal through the guise of his dead spouse. In so doing, it succeeded in reconnecting its Spirit with the blood and breath of several other Mortals. Creating this Construct, it would now be capable of walking the Earth again after millennia, released from the Hell of its imprisonment.

My thoughts reeled, dizzying. They kept switching from the Cat's to my own. I leapt into the air, claws extended as the Construct below me continued to mash up Clive's remains.

I had one chance … The Cat had one last chance …

With my full weight – the Cat's weight – behind me, my front claws speared the Construct above the grinding mouth, and my rear claws sliced through the lower part. Blood sprayed, black muck oozed. Stitches recoiled and whipped the air, dangling free.

And in a frenzy, with fiery energy crackling from my claws, I tore into the patchwork flesh.

Destroy the Construct.

More stitches snapped as the grisly flesh came apart in stringy clumps. I shredded and sliced and ravaged the Construct, tearing it into meaty sections. My growl intensified as the flaming energies trailed through my hair, along my paws.

In a bloody mess, the Daemon and Construct writhed; a collage of flesh and blood and ephemeral translucence. It slumped into itself, and its shriek drilled into my brain.

This Daemon will not rise. Ever.

The ground cracked underneath us as traces of that energy leaked into the mud. Still my claws ripped through stitches and chunks of fat and muscle, detaching the segments of broken bones and deformed cartilage.

Around us the shadows gaped, stretching, enveloping, and more of that energy sputtered around us. The Fabric opened up, a darkness strengthening, all encompassing, a vastness, a Black completely not of the Earth, stretched below and above, reaching from Stone to Stone.

And I sank.

Black Cat, Construct, Daemon … and Mortal.

Darkness stole away the last of the flames. The remaining Sigil Stones crumbled. Plumes of dust mixed with the smoky air and roiling fog.

The great void took me.

Into Beneath.

The feeling of being on my own ... of being mere *human* again ... was like a punch to the gut. That feeling of loss made me sink into the mud I lay in. Leo crouched over me. Beside him the Witchblade was stabbed in the ground.

"You okay?" he asked.

Light pained my eyes. Moonlight. No more fire. No more shadows. No more Construct. Faint mist crawled through tufts of grass and mounds of earth. I grabbed him and he winced; I held his wounded arm. I wanted to apologise but my throat hurt. It tasted of smoke and heat, of blood and decay. Gently, I released his arm and sat up. My head reeled in flashes. I could still feel the tingle of energy.

Or was that my imagination?

No more stones loomed over us, no more blackened tree trunks, although the earth was still upheaved in places. A few fragments of rock were scattered around, but all were unmarked. Certainly, none glowed. Ordinary rocks. There weren't even any shadows mingling with the fog. Beneath the white moonlight, the area had returned to normal. Plus, the atmosphere no longer felt tainted.

"You okay?" Leo repeated.

I nodded as I peered into the shadows of a faraway treeline. I wondered if the Black Cat was still around. Although ... I knew it was now *Beneath* with the Demon.

Something nudged my hand. I looked down.

"Hey, little man," I said.

Murphy nuzzled up against my leg and purred. He licked my fingers, his rough tongue cleaning filth from my knuckles.

LEO'S LAST WORD

Two weeks later

Leo stood out on the road watching Anne manoeuvre off her driveway and past the For-Sale sign. She waved out the window as she drove up the lane. He noticed the sunshine glint off her grandmother's ring, which she now wore. She deserved to leave Mabley Holt and better her life, but for him he had much more ahead.

Once her car disappeared round the bend, he walked across the road and onto the bridleway. With troubled thoughts, he emerged out the other side and headed for Pippa's gate instead of his own. For the briefest of moments, he considered turning back and going home.

He knocked, waited a few seconds, and dug in a pocket for the key.

Behind him out on the road, a delivery van shot past. He looked over his shoulder, hearing branches scrape down the bodywork as the van drifted into the bushes. It jerked and straightened up. Bits of leaves and twigs scattered across the road in its wake. The prick was on his mobile.

"Pippa, it's me," he called as he opened the door. He stepped into the warm house with that familiar smell of acrylics, and Georgie came to greet him. He closed the door and crouched to stroke the dog.

"How's it going, Georgie?"

Together, the pair went through the house and into the studio.

"Hello." Pippa didn't turn. As always, she faced a canvas. "Did Anne get away safely?"

"Yeah," Leo said as he leaned against the doorframe. "Murphy is adorable. It was great to see the pair reunited. She wanted to say goodbye, you know."

"I know."

"We could have told her more."

"I know."

"Much more," Leo added and scratched his beard. He'd not shaved for two weeks.

Pippa turned and looked at him from the shadow of her hoodie. "Anne's been through enough without looking at this." She gestured to her face with a brush.

It was Leo's turn to say, "I know."

"This is my Hell."

As always, the face Pippa once had teased his perception. Some days it was better than others. Today, her face hid behind wavering shadowy folds and mottled skin. Hundreds of thin veins crisscrossed beneath the tight flesh where her eyes and mouth should've been, and just two small holes remained where her nose was. With only a hint of those once-pretty features, it reminded him of looking underwater where everything is blurred and unfocussed. Soon, in one of his books, he'd find something to help her. Somehow.

"You eaten?" he asked. He'd seen how she had to eat. Mainly junk food, lots of microwavable meals, that kind of shit. Mind you, his diet wasn't too great these days either. He marvelled at how easily she'd accepted it, how she had to wait for her mouth to reappear so she can quickly force food down. And the fact that she was still able to talk to him when her mouth vanished. How was that even possible?

Mental.

This whole game was mental.

"I ate a little earlier," she said and dunked her brush in some black paint. Too often black.

As for Anne: she'd been through Hell in so many ways, and Leo knew that although they'd banished that one demon, there were many others that would attempt to pass through the Fabric. Anne deserved a new life elsewhere. Indeed, she deserved much more than the life he and Pippa led.

Leo watched the artist do what she did best.

"The Shadow Fabric is still proving to be a bitch," he said.

A BONUS STORY

Something that happened the year before

THE ARTIST AND THE CRONE

I guess there will always be something in Mabley Holt to keep me here. Even after all the crazy stuff back in the spring, I returned and bought this tiny cottage with its equally tiny garden hemmed in by a precarious ragstone wall. As a man of little needs this was a perfect place to settle.

Perhaps it was stupid to think things wouldn't catch me up.

My one neighbour whose cottage was marginally larger than my own was a young lady of a similar age to me, with a reserved smile. If I thought my garden needed attention – those nettles were tall enough to sting your face – hers was equally neglected. We'd acknowledged each other when I'd moved in and that had been it.

After three weeks and kind of settled in, I dozed in front of a late night TV programme. A scream jerked me upright. On my feet, I staggered. That shrill cry still echoed, if not through the house but through my head. I yanked open the front door and stepped into the night. A cold moon pushed down on me just as the cold paving pressed up into the soles of my feet. I ran towards my neighbour's house. The place was silent and dark.

She'd had a nightmare, that was all. I headed back inside to bed.

Morning came and I awoke to the sound of thumps and clatters as though someone threw things in temper. I leapt from bed and raked fingers through my hair. Pulling aside the curtains without thought of my nakedness, I glared out the window and into her garden.

Dressed in a paint-spattered jumper and jeans, my neighbour stood beside a wheelie-bin. Its lid was up and rested against the ivy-shrouded fence. She was upending a number of shoeboxes and cartons, pouring out paint bottles and brushes and all manner of art supplies. Swiping away her dishevelled hair, she stepped backwards and looked up.

At me.

I twisted sideways, suddenly realising how naked I was, and the edge of the dresser stabbed my spine. She must've seen me. I waited, my back pressed to the cold wood. By the time I leaned sideways and peaked around the curtains, her garden was empty. She hadn't even put the bin lid down.

The day came and went; a day that I spent reading. Recently, I'd been reading a lot. All the books I'd inherited, books that truly belonged in a museum, were a mine of information that I hoped would help me understand a little piece of my troubled past. I'd even thumbed through a few books relating to local witch trials – it seemed Mabley Holt hadn't escaped witchcraft back in the 17th century, and given the small dealings I previously had with a magic that was most definitely black, that came as no surprise. The Shadow Fabric, a sentient darkness, was perhaps the most blackest of the arts imaginable.

Having just finished dinner, I heard my neighbour scream again. Only this time much closer, from outside perhaps. I took the stairs two at a time and ran into my bedroom, to the window. She stood in her garden, her face illuminated by the roaring flames from a twisted, shrunken bin. Thick smoke corkscrewed upwards.

Back downstairs again, I snatched my boots and yanked them on. One was bulkier now I'd modified it to conceal a weapon – these days I was always prepared. Keeping the Witchblade to hand was comforting, and as far as I could tell it was the only one in existence. I yanked open the back gate and ran alongside her house, over cracked paving and brambles threatening to trip me. The crackle of flames was louder as I approached. I stumbled into her garden. The stink of plastic and chemicals stung my nostrils.

Dressed in the same paint-splashed jumper as when I'd seen her that morning, she threw me a glance then looked back at the fire. Flames roared. Spirals of grey-black smoke reached the twilight clouds.

She scanned her garden. I guessed she looked for something to put out the fire. If we could contain it fast enough we'd not need the fire brigade. I ran over to where a hose coiled, tangled with grass.

"This attached to anything?" I shouted.

She nodded, hair catching in her mouth. She hooked it out.

"Turn it on!"

She seemed doubtful for a moment. I dragged the hose closer to the flames as she vanished round the corner. Heat prickled my face. The hose jerked, spat, then hissed a stream of water and I directed the nozzle around the edge of the inferno. Smoke belched and I cupped a hand over my mouth and nose. Waving the hose left and right, I doused the flames and gradually worked inwards. Defiant at first, the fire diminished.

Eventually, I stood back but kept the hose aimed at the dirty rainbow of molten colours. Several fence panels showed a few scorch marks. The ivy had burnt away and water dripped from the shrivelled and blackened ends.

"Reckon you can turn it off now," I said.

Her face, although relieved, seemed to shrink. Her mouth slightly open, she disappeared round the corner again. I heard a couple of squeaks and finally the flow dribbled. She returned just as the last drip splashed my boot.

"I'm Leo," I said.

"Pippa," she whispered, "and thank you."

I coiled the hose in a pathetic attempt at neatness, and dropped it on a rusted garden chair. My cuff had ridden halfway up my forearm and something made me quickly tug it down to hide the mark, the scar – I've called it a scar all along but I've always known it was more than that.

For something to say, I said, "Guess you're an artist."

"I wish I wasn't."

"That why you threw all that stuff out?"

"Yep." Tears welled in her eyes and she glanced away, wiping them.

"Flammable, that stuff."

She held one hand in the other, squeezing her thumb. "Thank you."

"You've already said that."

A weak smile pushed into her moist cheeks.

"W—" I began.

Something crashed from inside her house. It sounded like deckchairs collapsing all at once.

"Not again!" Pippa yelled and ran indoors.

I followed, unable to work out whether I'd seen fear or anger in her face.

We entered the kitchen first. The aroma of fresh coffee overwhelmed me. Plates and cutlery were stacked high in a sink filled with filthy water, and a scatter of cornflakes covered the counter. Into the hallway next. The layout was similar to my own and where my back room had become a library, she'd converted hers into a studio. Or at least it seemed her intention; the carpet was half rolled across the room to reveal the floorboards.

Pippa flicked the light switch but nothing happened. Desperation made her try again. And again. On, off. On, off. Click. Click. Click …

"Stop it," I told her.

The final click echoed and fell into the silence.

Evidently this was where the noise had come from.

A shrinking evening light cast a blue haze into the room. Five canvasses of varying sizes were strewn across the bare floorboards in the jagged clutches of splintered easels. Paint of all colours had soaked into the pile and peppered the floorboards. Bottles and brushes were all over the place. The black was still spreading, flowing between floorboards.

Pippa's hands twisted together. "I've so many deadlines approaching."

I didn't know what to say.

"And then all this crap happens." She squeezed tight her eyelids. "I can't handle this."

She had skill, yet the content was questionable. One painting depicted a landscape; hills and fields and a brooding sky. In the foreground an oak tree loomed over the bodies of men, their tunics clawed open around red and ragged wounds. The way some of those men held themselves suggested not all were dead. Blood soaked the grass. From a gnarled branch above dangled a woman dressed in rags, her neck broken and hooked in a noose. Such was the detail you could hear the men groan, the rope creak, and almost see the woman's body swing.

Another was of a village market square. A crowd gathered around a pyre, its flames licking the night. At its heart, thrashed an elderly woman tied to a wooden post. In the shadows at the rear of the crowd, several men writhed on the uneven paving, their faces a bloody mess. Again, such was Pippa's skill I heard the crackling flames, the woman's screams.

The other paintings depicted similar scenes of women dying; drowned, stabbed, beheaded. The latter was particularly gruesome.

I had no doubt as to who or what these women were: witches. After all that happened to me at the beginning of the year, was I again dealing with witches?

"Please don't judge me." Pippa's voice drifted over my

shoulder.

I pushed fingers through my hair. It was getting long and I realised I hadn't had it cut for over a year.

"I know what you're thinking," she continued, "but I don't usually paint this kind of shit."

"You have no idea what I'm thinking."

She picked red paint from her cuff.

"Let's put it this way," I added, "I have books that delve into the history of witchcraft. I'm talking about a real history you won't find anywhere in your local library. Or online."

She crouched and pulled a canvas towards her. It was the one of a woman's limp body being dragged up a riverbank by whom I suspected to be the Witchfinder General himself – a man who in the 17th century unceremoniously tortured women suspected of witchcraft. He was beneath the shadowy arc of a bridge. The darkness that clutched the stonework churned as though sentient, its coiled tendrils extending towards the cheering men above.

Together, Pippa and I propped the canvasses against the wall and set aside the splintered easels. Her work really was good. There was something about the way she used subtle brush strokes around the figures that gave the impression of motion. There must be a technical term for it but I wasn't an art critic. She had talent, that much was obvious.

Then I found a sixth canvas, smaller than the others. My hands froze.

"What is it?" Her voice was tiny.

I stared at the painting. Of all of them, this one was unfinished – or at least appeared to be. It was a landscape focused around a wall of looming rock, moss-covered and ancient. In their shadowy embrace, dark clumps of what appeared to be fungus covered the leaf-strewn ground. But on the rock, the symbol – the *sigil*, as I'd recently learned – was barely noticeable yet it was there like some prehistoric cave painting. Faded red, a symbol of two triangles facing one another, one hollow, the other solid, and separated by a crude X.

"Leo?"

I touched my sleeve – an unconscious habit now. I should've known this would never end.

I relaxed my jaw. "These are good."

"What is it?" She demanded, her voice now even smaller.

"I …"

"You recognise it." Her chin quivered. "That symbol."

"Yes."

"What does it mean?"

"Pippa, I—"

Behind us, the floorboards creaked.

Timber groaned and split and heaved as though something pushed from beneath. Nails pinged around us. Pippa shrieked and ducked, and something stung my cheek. From between splitting planks, a cluster of shadows bubbled. Like liquid it oozed upwards and stretched as though testing the air. Faint strands coiled and whipped, spraying flecks of darkness like black tentacles flicking ink.

"What's happening?" Pippa shouted.

From my boot, I pulled out the Witchblade.

She stumbled backwards, wide eyed. She stared at the spreading darkness – those sentient shadows I was all-too-familiar with – and then back to the curved blade in my hand. "Leo?"

I stood between her and the shadows, pointing the blade towards the expanding darkness. Already the tip spat white energy. That ozone smell – something I'd almost forgotten – teased my senses, somehow comforting. This reassurance of its power was short-lived however, as the oppression of the shadows constricted not only the light but peace of mind, sanity, anything *positive*. It made me want to turn the blade on myself, to push its length through my jacket, to feel my intestines slice open … The warmth, the freedom …

I shook my head. "No!"

Pippa shuddered. By the look on her face she was having equally disturbing thoughts. She glared at me.

The shadows thickened and a thin tendril shot towards us, towards me. It snatched the Witchblade from my hand. I grabbed air as the shadow snaked back into the growing nest of darkness.

"That was not supposed to happen," I said. There'd been a time when the shadows were afraid of the damn thing.

Pippa had pushed herself against a far wall. "None of this is supposed to happen."

As though holding their breath, the shadows sucked inward and released the weapon. With a glint of fading daylight, the blade thumped an angled floorboard. It spun, then slid and came to rest on one of the straighter, untouched boards.

I started forward, reaching out.

"Don't!" Pippa screamed.

The Witchblade twitched and jumped and landed again with a clunk. As though an invisible hand grabbed it, the blade stabbed the timber … then scraped along the grain. Wood curled in its wake, nearing the spilled black paint.

My lungs tightened. All the books I'd read since the chaos at Periwick House, the sentient darkness of the Shadow Fabric, the reanimated dead, the deaths of those I'd known … all I'd learned during and after that time, was useless. These shadows were different. Sentient as before, but this was something else. And when the blade – my Witchblade – dipped into the paint and began to write, I knew this was entirely something else.

H …

"What the—?" I shouted.

H … E …

Pippa pushed herself against me, tugging my jacket.

HELP.

What the hell was going on?

ME.

"Leo?" Pippa whispered.

The blade clanked to the floor, spun once, and was still.

HELP ME.

The heaviness in the room somehow weakened, my brain clearing. Whatever supernatural Being was behind this had apparently spent its energy. The darkness had fully retreated, to bubble like a pool beneath the split floorboards. It seethed, spitting shadows like puffs of smoke.

I stepped forward and pulled Pippa with me – she still had my jacket in her hands.

"Um, sorry." She let go and straightened, seeming taller. She was still about a foot shorter than me.

Spreading my stance, I grabbed the Witchblade. Nothing happened.

She eyed the weapon.

"Let's get out of here." I told her. I didn't know what else to say, what else to do. This was her home certainly, but what could we do? And who the hell had written that message?

Once again the floorboards creaked and heaved, though not as fierce as before. Rusted nails screeched. The darkness oozed from beneath and streaked across the wood, stretched over the skirting and up the wall. It spread like damp blemishes, only thick and black.

I nudged Pippa towards the doorway. "Go!"

The door slammed just before we reached it.

Pippa actually laughed. "Of course."

More darkness blossomed. We backed up. The window was our only exit. I glanced around for something heavy enough to smash it. I went to grab an easel, and …

In a surge of shadow and brick and mortar, a portion of wall burst outwards into the garden. Twilight and cold air rushed in. Brick dust swirled. Dry, bitter.

I looked back at the door. The darkness spread across the wall and over the door panel, the knob vanishing in a twist of shadow. Whether this was a supernatural entity or even the Shadow Fabric, it seemed we had only one exit. I left the easel where it was.

"Go!" I shoved her towards the heaped masonry. "Now!"

She staggered and I gripped her shoulder, steadying her. My neck tingled, feeling the encroaching darkness. Rubble shifted beneath our feet and we made it into the garden. The Witchblade was still in my hand yet there was no energy coming from it. Cold and useless.

I had no idea where to go.

Further ahead, separating our gardens, the ragstone wall exploded. Dust and darkness bloomed, the grass heaved. Deep-rooted shadows churned in the crumbled remains. I'd seen this before, back when I'd witnessed the Shadow Fabric burst from the ground. Yet this was different, *everything* that was happening was different.

At some point I'd grabbed Pippa's hand. She was cold. For a moment I thought of heading for my house but that was absurd; there'd be no safety so close.

From the edges of uprooted ground, like some kind of black fungus, dark streaks broke across the grass, curling and bursting and mixing with the earth. Sweaty, glistening heads bulged and split, oozing black goo and bleeding into the shadows.

This was most definitely different than anything else I'd experienced.

Pippa's hand wrenched from my grip and I staggered.

She was no longer there.

I scanned the collected shadows, natural or otherwise. More of that fungus smothered the grass and weeds, choking foliage.

Her cry echoed from somewhere ahead. I stepped sideways, forward and back. Where the hell—

Beyond the crumbled wall, along the row of trees that marked the surrounding fields, a cluster of shadow thickened. Beneath over-hanging branches, Pippa's face, pale and wide eyed, stared back at me.

Her muffled cry of "Leo!" echoed as though even further away.

I leapt over the sprouting fungus. How had she travelled so far? I sprinted. Almost there, and … her body stretched with the darkness, her form rotating, churning like curdled milk. She vanished. Only to appear again further away, past the trees and in the fields. More fungus spread, and again she cried out.

I charged towards her, my arms pumping close to my body, my feet slamming hard on the uneven ground. The Witchblade spat weak pulses of energy, somehow depleted. Having been touched by the shadows, perhaps its power had been drained. I had no time to think on it.

Again in a blur of black and white her image phased into an almost ghost-like streak. Then vanished. Still I ran. How many more times will she vanish and reappear? Finally to be lost altogether? Tall grass whipped my legs. Up ahead, the sweaty heads of fungus glistened in the fading light as if to guide my way.

Pippa's silhouette ricocheted from tree to tree, merging with the shadows. Shimmering images of her leapt from shadow to shadow, across fields, appearing and disappearing. Again and again … Her screams were muted; a constant echo.

Still, I ran.

Up a gradual rise, her image flashed yet again. It clung

to the natural shadows between trees. Faint at first, then her terrified face sharpened, bright in contrast to the seething darkness that trapped her.

"Help me!"

Her words reminded me of the message written in her studio. Was that Pippa who now screamed it or was it whoever had used the Witchblade to write in the paint?

She vanished.

My breath short, I made it to the tree line. More fungus ate into the foliage to mark the way. I kept the trees to my left and charged past. Into another field. Up ahead, a jagged outline cut the deep blue of twilight sky. Once a barn or some kind of outhouse, crumbled walls hid in a sea of nettles and tangled brambles. A corrugated roof, rusted and buckled, lay beneath heaped bricks and rotten timber. The fungus, the thickened shadows, ended.

There was Pippa. But—

No, it couldn't be her.

Wisps of shadow drifted over the brickwork, blending with a dozen images of her sitting on the ruined walls.

Closer, and I saw it wasn't Pippa but several different women dressed in rags or long skirts, filthy and sodden. A storm of shadow obscured their heads, hiding their faces. One had a noose around her neck while another sat cradling her arm. Another held a bundle of rags close to her bosom, perhaps a child. One of the women, whose hair dripped a liquid darkness, kicked at a black mess at her feet.

My pace slowed. I had no doubt these women were witches. Whether practitioners of black or white witchcraft, they were here. *Ghosts* of witches, and Pippa had painted their deaths.

I jogged to a halt.

As if to acknowledge me, their limbs jerked. Excited almost. Their heads swayed with the darkness that hid their faces. Wisps of shadow skittered around them, teasing. In turn, the darkness fell from their heads. Faceless. Framed by unkempt hair, their smooth and mottled flesh stretched blank where faces should be. Stretched like a canvas. Dark veins bulged ready to burst from the skin. One had her hair tied back in a red scarf, though most left it straggly and knotted. Others kept it long. But their faces. Holy shit, their faces. Or lack of.

I tightened my grip on the Witchblade and approached.

Fungus crawled up the brickwork, teasing the mortar. The black vines brushed one of the women's dangling bare feet.

As I neared the ruin, I saw Pippa. Finally.

Across an expanse of swaying nettles, Pippa slumped against crumbled brickwork. Of all the women here, she was the only one whose image was sharp, clear. She hunched in shadows that appeared to boil from the ground, her arms outstretched and bound by loops of darkness. It was like she was crucified.

I rushed forward and tripped. My knees thumped the ground.

Around me, a deepening darkness twisted and uprooted clumps of earth. Vines as thick as my forearm snaked upwards, daring me to approach further. The trunks split and black spores puffed, clouding the air.

I held my breath and scrambled up. There was no way I wanted to inhale that crap. I backed off. Shadows thickened, blackening the grass and spreading further to the left and right. More vines twisted with the earth, their lengths splitting open with tiny mouths dribbling fungus and spores. Barbs pushed from beneath grey flesh, curved and wicked.

A wall of shadow swept up, blocking my advance.

I thrust with the Witchblade. The blade sliced through the darkness and when I yanked it out, the jagged tear sucked closed again. There was no Witchblade fire, no power or strength to be gained when brandishing it; I may as well have been holding a dinner knife.

I took another step back as those vines slithered towards me. Those barbs looked nasty. Spore clouds drifted.

"Why the hell did you lead me here?" I yelled beneath my hand as I clamped it around my nose and mouth.

A torrent of shadow roared above the ruined walls, blending with the onset of night, obscuring a moon desperate to break through the clouds. Amid the roiling darkness, images flickered like TV screens. Each showed another place, another time.

"What is this?" I demanded.

… a swinging noose from an oak tree …

"Tell me!"

… deep water and flailing limbs …

Pippa's scream echoed, muted in the darkness. "Leo!"

… blood pouring from wounds along a slender arm pricked with needles and sliced with daggers …

Memories. Each mirrored Pippa's paintings to reveal the suffering and individual deaths of these women. Perhaps they were innocent of witchcraft or were even white witches, never using their craft for the dark arts.

As one, these phantoms raised an arm. Clumps of shadow and filth dripped from sleeves. They pointed at Pippa.

Still I couldn't advance, couldn't help her. She struggled in the embrace of a thickening darkness, stitched into the shadows. She writhed, jerking her head back and forth. "Leo!"

Beneath her the ground bulged.

I lunged forward and smaller vines whipped up. A billowing cloud of spores filled the air. And again, I backed off.

The ground shook and through the tangle of nettles near Pippa's kicking feet, a barbed trunk as thick as a telegraph pole burst upwards in an eruption of earth. The vine slumped against the wall, smashing through brick. Hundreds of barbs scraped the brickwork, rasping as they reached for her.

The scene brightened as moonlight finally peeked through the clouds. Its ambience weak yet managing to break through the darkness and roiling shadows.

It highlighted everything.

"Shit!" I shouted.

From the immense trunk, a barb had extended, longer than the others ... closer and closer towards Pippa ... and it pierced her wrist. Blood trickled.

Her scream filled my head.

Again, I charged forward and again the barrier forced me back. Pathetic sparks dripped from the Witchblade – still the damn thing was useless. Something was draining its energy.

One of the phantoms, her face glistening in the silver light of the moon, pointed to her wrist. The others stroked theirs, too. A few even nodded. Their freaky, faceless heads bobbed up and down in a stuttering blur. Even more grotesque now they were lit up by the moon.

"I can see that!" I shouted. I knew that barb had pierced Pippa's wrist. What did they want me to do?

A phantom shook her head.

"No?" This was insane. But fuck, I should be used to this.

The same phantom slapped her wrist, so hard I almost heard it. Slap-slap-slap-slapslap ... No, it wasn't her wrist, but her forearm.

"What?" Then I knew. I knew without a doubt what these dead witches referred to. I pulled back my sleeve to reveal a scar where once I was branded in the shape of the same sigil Pippa had painted.

I shouted at them, my voice a roar: "This?" I held up my arm. The skin itched and burned like fresh sunburn.

What precisely were these phantoms telling me?

Pippa still thrashed in the embrace of the shadows and coiled vines. Another barb had pressed into her other wrist, and blood trickled down her hands to drip from clawed fingers. Her clothes were filthy, smeared black with mud and fungus.

At her feet, in front of the slithering vines, the shadows bloomed and opened up.

An image flashed.

I blinked.

The unfolding darkness lightened and wavered like a poor-quality video. Then sharpened, in and out of focus to show something familiar: Pippa's scattered paintings and spilled paints. I watched as I had earlier, the Witchblade – the Witchblade from the *past* – write HELP ME. Only this time a ghostly hand visibly gripped its hilt, the knuckles gnarled and arthritic, liver-spotted and wrinkled. The image panned back to reveal the frail and hunched form of another witch. Her stained clothes, no more than rags bound by frayed rope, were caked in mud, thick like clay. Across thin shoulders draped a dark patchwork shawl, leathery and rumpled. She released the blade and as before, it dropped to the floorboards. The crone stepped back and turned and looked directly at me.

I jerked and coughed, and I hoped to hell I hadn't inhaled any of those spores – although their clouds had calmed now I'd stepped further back.

Tiny eyes, darker than the surrounding shadows, glared through a mass of spider-web hair. Her nose was a fleshy lump above the thin slit of a mouth that curled into a twist of scar tissue. Once upon a time she'd been burned. Badly. I thought of Pippa's market square painting; the one where the witch writhed in roaring flames. Was this her whose form now shimmered as she reached the edge of the shadows? Was this a portal?

The darkness shuddered. She stepped through into the present.

Shadows sucked at her and there she stood. Nettles smouldered and shrivelled, crumbled dead at her feet. Even the earth blackened. Smoke and shadow curled into the air. She lifted her head and eyed the Witchblade in my hand. Her lips twitched, the webbed scar silvering beneath the moonlight. Twitch-twitch, twitch. Was that a smile?

The Witchblade – the Witchblade of the *present* – jerked and a warmth spread up my arm. Traceries of white fire spat from the blade. Still its power was limited. I gripped tighter. The same white energy skittered across the crone's shawl, weaving with the stitches between each patchwork section. It seemed to writhe, charged with new power.

Then it all made sense.

"You crafty bitch," I shouted.

Already having sufficient power to snatch the Witchblade from me in Pippa's studio – somehow twisting time, too – this crone had harnessed its energy. Leading me here, she'd then channelled the energy so to transport herself from the death, the *hell*, she came. The way her form shifted and shivered, edges fuzzy one moment and sharp the next, suggested this was only part of her resurrection.

Another piece of this puzzle was Pippa.

She was still framed by the great hulks of vine, barbs secured into veins. Waves of shadow braced her shoulders and bound her arms. Her head lolled, her eyelids droopy as though she was drunk. Soft moans drifted towards me.

Seeing her like that made me feel so damn helpless.

The crone, of all the other witches, was undoubtedly the most powerful; evidently the only one present with such power to cheat death, even though she'd been burnt at the stake. Her shawl moved as though the wind was fiercer than it was. A patchwork of fabrics … brown, dark, stained. And it moved, contradicting the crone's own movements as she approached Pippa. It was alive, pulsing. *Breathing*. The darker patches reminded me of the Shadow Fabric, the way it shifted like spilled diesel. The crumpled sections, some kind of animal hide, had been stitched with it.

Then I knew precisely who this crone was. How she'd accomplished all this I hadn't a clue, but I had no doubt of her identity.

Belle Mayher. A woman who was said to have lived beyond the age of 250, noted to have stitched the largest sections of the Shadow Fabric. The very Fabric that would later be unleashed across London in 1666, before the Great Fire. Her powers were unparalleled and included the unique ability to absorb others' powers and abilities. She had been – still was? – in league with an entity known as Clay, Demon Stitcher of Shadow and Skin. Human skin, not animal hide (to demons we *are* animals). Selling your soul was not a myth; she'd done precisely that. And she wore proof to the fact.

I could only assume she was at this very moment absorbing Pippa's artistic skills. To what gains, I had no idea. I knew for certain, however, she was even now absorbing the Witchblade energy; that's why its power was weak.

A cold wind bit through my clothes and I shivered.

The other phantoms had retreated. Some huddled against each other. The one with the baby shook uncontrollably. Fungus grew from the rags she cradled. The closest phantom whose feet dripped dark water, frantically waved her forearm and it was as if I heard her yell for my attention … even though she had no mouth. She made sawing motions across her forearm.

Was she telling me to cut myself?

I raised the Witchblade.

She stopped sawing and her faceless head jerked in affirmation. Dark splashes flicked upwards.

I didn't want to cut myself, that was absurd. My scar, shaped like an hourglass, had become part of me and this dead witch wanted me to cut it. Not a day had passed when I didn't drag my fingertips over the lumpy twists of skin, thinking, remembering … I guessed I'd always be connected to the darkness that we humans are so ignorant towards. It's always been there, and always will be.

The crone, Mayher, had grasped Pippa's head in one hand and a barbed vine in the other. Blood gushed from her serrated palm. Her lips moved, chanting some witchcraft bullshit. Her shawl surged and writhed about her shoulders, energised.

Moonlight reflected from the blade I held before me. I could only guess that cutting myself would somehow reenergise the Witchblade, to steal the power back from Mayher. I pressed it, warm, vibrating, against the scar and quickly sliced along the outer edge of the sigil.

A thin line blossomed red, oozing. Entirely painless.

From across the ruins, the crone's dark gaze struck me. My hand froze. Her lips peeled back over broken teeth and she hissed louder than the wind.

Now I bled, having done what I'd been instructed – advised by a dead witch, for God's sake – what the hell was I supposed to do now?

I lifted my arm and shook it.

Blood spattered and disappeared onto the blackened ground.

The fungus quivered, the grey heads lightening, breaking apart. I waved my arm around, the blood pouring out – worryingly a little more than I'd hoped. But it worked. The fungus shrivelled and crumbled. Swiftly, quicker than I would've expected, the clumps dissolved. The air no longer tasted as tainted as before, and I stepped forward over the dead ground. Blood dripped down my forearm, my fingers now slick.

Pippa's body no longer moved. I hoped I wasn't too late.

The shadows had even retreated.

"Ha!" I yelled into the swirling masses as they drifted away.

I ran towards Pippa and Mayher. Fungus puffed into harmless dust beneath my pounding boots. The nettles and brambles and grass broke away with the crumbling fungus, leaving dead ground, mud and dirt.

The crone's scar twisted ugly and she glared at me, eyes a wicked Stygian darkness. Her shawl seethed around her shoulders, the patches squirming and glistening. She shrieked.

It drilled into my brain and I staggered. Colourful zigzags pressed in on my vision, threatening to yank me into the shrivelled tangles of blackened nettles and grass. Witchblade fire spat and charged, red and orange and yellow flares lit my way. Finally, I had control; I had the blade's power back in hand. My muscles flexed and I straightened.

Still Mayher shrieked, hunched and buckled over as the faint energy drifted across her shoulders and down to clawed hands. White charges spat from her fingertips. She'd lost control of that stolen power.

I leapt and booted her in the chest.

My foot passed through her … but slammed into the shawl. It flew from her and slapped the brickwork. It fell, twitching in the still-dissolving fungus.

Mayher staggered backwards as though I'd succeeded in kicking her. Her ephemeral form shifted and slid from focus, merging and churning with the broiling darkness. Her shriek was now dampened, subdued by the retreating shadows. Through weak, grey eyes she looked down at her shawl.

Part-flesh, part-shadow, the foul garment writhed on the ground. Patchwork sections had come undone and the flesh seethed, rippled. Blood oozed from torn stitches, and frayed ends of shadow squirmed as though desperate to be threaded once more.

Defying the shadows that embraced her, Mayher rushed for me. The darkness shredded.

She yelled and swiped at me.

I crouched and swung my arm up to block, ready to thrust with the Witchblade. Her gnarled fingers passed through me.

Hair rose on the back of my neck.

Behind her, the darkness thickened. Dense tendrils whipped around her neck and torso to snatch her backwards, her heels digging into the ground yet leaving no mark. Her eyes flared. The shadows were determined to take her back into death. She struggled, throwing glances at her shawl that bled into the cracked earth.

Pippa still hadn't moved. Still the barbs were rooted in her veins. The shadows that bound her wrists drifted away yet the vine held her upright. They hadn't dissolved with the rest of the fungus. Being as trunk-like as they were, I guessed they'd be the last to respond to whatever power my blood contained. This was new to me; all this was a different kind of weird.

I reached Pippa and stabbed those massive trunks. Witchblade fire, white and brilliant, rushed towards the barbs that punctured her skin. Black filth bubbled and oozed from the wounds and the barbs slid free. Harmless to us, the fire roared and enveloped the trunks. The thick flesh blistered, stinking and smouldering. They thumped the ground and deflated, shrivelling into twisted coils of muck.

Pippa flopped into my arms. I propped her against the wall. Her eyelids flickered and she murmured something.

Mayhar's scream pulled me upright.

The phantoms were all now animated, their faceless heads turned to the crone as she kicked at the shadows. The other witches were clearly fearful of Mayher which led me to believe she'd somehow collected them here to reinforce her resurrection. I could only assume she'd absorbed their abilities and crafts even in death.

Mayher had somehow reached her shawl, now clutching its patchwork remains together. Gore dripped from it in clumps, black threads dangling.

I jumped up. Witchblade fire erupted from the blade and I rushed towards her as again she attempted to strike me. A darkness flickered behind her eyes as though energised once again by the shawl. White energy flared from the blade and shot into her face. Again, this witch burned. 350 years beyond her death, after a failed resurrection, fire ate into her skin once again; Witchblade fire she failed to control.

Her scream tore through the countryside.

I swiped the blade downwards into the shawl. It sliced through the fabric. Shadows bubbled and flesh bled. The crone retreated. She flailed, desperate to hold on to the garment. Again the shadows snatched at her.

Pippa was pushing herself to unsteady feet.

"Go!" I shouted at her.

She scrubbed the blood and filth from her arms and succeeded only in smearing it. Her hair obscured her face.

The shadows were diminishing, and the fungus shrank to become little more than grey goo. So too were the remaining vines, crumbling to dust.

The phantoms whipped the shadows into clouds and as one, they swarmed Mayher. A blur of ghostly rags and skinny limbs flew down on the crone. Glimmers of faces, eyes and noses and mouths appeared – some of them were attractive, or had been in their day. Pretty faces, whether innocent of witchcraft, whether practitioners of white or black arts, they had been released. No longer were they the forgotten faces of the 17th-century witch trials.

Mayher struggled beneath the onslaught of phantoms and deeper shadows that surged around them all. A wall shook and collapsed in a rush of brick dust and lingering shadow. I had no idea what the ground would do given that the fungus was shrivelling and the vines crumbled.

"Run!" That word had become too familiar. Ever since the evil behind the shadows had returned, ever since the hell that had occurred at Periwick House, I'd shouted that a lot.

So we ran. With a final glance over my shoulder, I saw Mayher and the phantoms vanish in a vortex of shadow.

Moonlight swamped the area, cleaner, fresher. A dust cloud caught on the wind.

We sprinted across the fields. When we were safe, I looked at Pippa.

Just like the phantoms, she had no face.

The Artist and the Crone ©Mark Cassell 2015, Herbs House
previously published in SINISTER STITCHES

THE SHADOW FABRIC

Novel extract

Unable to blink, I shot a quick glance around the dining room. My heartbeat stormed my head. I had to get out of there, I had to leave the other men to it. These brothers had a lot of hate to throw around.

The black fabric draped across the table and chair, tracing every contour. It flowed over the wood like liquid. Hugging tight whatever it touched, it turned everything into a shadow, a silhouette, a featureless dark blot of its former self. The way it moved defied physics.

My throat clamped around a cry that came out a whimper.

I had no idea what Stanley intended. The strange fabric didn't travel far from his hand, and where the material ended, it rippled and pulsed, pulling further away, yet unable to claim more of its surroundings. The more it unfolded, the dimmer the room became. My skin itched as it sapped the light.

Victor and Stanley stood facing each other: Victor, with his eyebrows pushed together, the ornate blade clenched in a fist, and Stanley, with his jaw tight and a twitch at the edge of his mouth. In Stanley's grasp the fabric quivered, its material reminding me of the way midday sunlight reflects from the surface of a swimming pool, the ripples a criss-crossing of movement. It was peaceful to behold, hypnotic almost. But this thing was dark and stifling to observe.

There was nothing remotely tranquil about this.

I wanted to leave them to whatever absurd game this was…yet my feet refused to move. The familiar ache in my knee rushed through my body, drumming in my skull, telling me I was useless. Since the car accident the knee often was useless. I couldn't leave Victor, I knew that. The man looked as terrified as I felt.

"I hate you, Victor." Stanley's nose was no more than a thumb's width from his brother's.

"No," Victor gasped. His hand shook, his knuckles whitening around the knife. "Don't!"

I didn't know who or what Victor spoke to. Was it Stanley? The shadows? The knife?

In a blur of darkness, shadows coiling his arm, the blade slammed into Stanley's chest. Blood spread and he staggered back.

Victor's eyes widened. Clutching the weapon, he stumbled from the fireplace, away from his brother. The knife slid out, sucking at the wound. A jet of scarlet misted the air, and then oozed.

I could only see darkness…so much darkness, and my lungs went tight.

The fabric—the Shadow Fabric—closed around Stanley's buckling legs.

The remaining material swept from the table, away from the violin case. Black tentacles whipped and grabbed Stanley. The darkness enfolded him as his eyes glazed over. It dragged his body along the carpet a short distance and tightened its grip.

My jaw muscles twitched as I clenched my teeth.

The Fabric began to shrink. Still in its embrace, the last I saw of Stanley was his dead stare.

"Vic…" I whispered, and gripped the back of the sofa.

My boss dragged his eyes away from the retreating shadows and stared at the knife. Behind him, the mantel clock hammered out several seconds before the weapon slipped from his hand onto the carpet, where it bounced with a red splash.

He fell to his knees. "Oh God."

The Fabric vanished.

I dashed across the room as much as my leg would allow and staggered to a halt beside him. Sobs wracked his frame as I grasped his bony shoulder.

On the table next to where Stanley had been standing was the violin case, still open like a crooked yawn.

A million thoughts tumbled through my head, but I couldn't find the words. I'd been Victor's chauffeur for no more than a day, and already I'd witnessed him stab his own brother. What the hell?

I don't know how long I remained like that, holding him, with light creeping reluctantly back into the room. Victor shouldn't have been surprised that the shadows had taken his brother. After all, those shadows—the darkness—are associated with all that is dead…or should be dead.

Silence clogged the air like we were buried in a tomb.

For some of us, there is a moment in our lives where all we've believed real is whipped out from under us and we're left to survive in a world that's a lie. All the things in life we've taken for granted are sheathed in a weak veneer, behind which stands the shadows.

For me, this was one of those moments.

ACKNOWLEDGEMENTS

First up, I have to thank Nev Murray for his help with just about everything from character names to promotion. Also, a huge thank you to Miranda Boers for her valuable advice with the tangled mess of my early draft. Without her help, I'd perhaps still be quivering in the shadows.

ABOUT THE AUTHOR

Mark Cassell lives in a rural part of the UK where he often dreams of dystopian futures, peculiar creatures, and flitting shadows. Primarily a horror writer, his steampunk, dark fantasy, and SF stories have featured in several anthologies and ezines. His best-selling debut novel THE SHADOW FABRIC is closely followed by the popular short story collection SINISTER STITCHES and are both only a fraction of an expanding mythos of demons, devices, and deceit.

Mark's 2017 release HELL CAT OF THE HOLT further explores the Shadow Fabric mythos with ghosts and black cat legends.

The dystopian sci-fi short story collection CHAOS HALO 1.0: ALPHA BETA GAMMA KILL is in association with Future Chronicles Photography where he works closely with their models and cosplayers.

For one of Mark's FREE stories go to:
www.markcassell.com

Or visit the website:
www.theshadowfabric.co.uk

THE SHADOW FABRIC

MARK CASSELL

Available in paperback and digital from Herbs House

Made in the USA
Columbia, SC
27 January 2018